EDGE OF DISASTER

AN EMP POST-APOCALYPTIC SURVIVAL PREPPER SERIES

ALEX GUNWICK

Cover Design by Jacqueline Sweet

He continued down the street. As he passed the kid, the worn face of an older man appeared behind the screen door. He held a shotgun at his side. Luke focused his peripheral vision on the man. If the shotgun so much as twitched, Luke would draw on him.

This wasn't the same world he'd left a week ago. This wasn't a world of business meetings and kids' soccer games. It was a world without rule of law. A world without mercy. A world without hope. And somehow, he had to survive it.

When he reached the end of the block, he risked a backward glance. The man stood on the front lawn. He held the shotgun in one hand, and his son's hand in the other. Luke's jaw twitched. He would have given anything to be able to hold his own son's hand. He couldn't do a damn thing to keep his family safe until he reached them. The weight of protecting their children rested solely on his wife Liz's shoulders. She was more than capable of handling herself, but he still worried.

Please let them be safe.

Luke continued through the neighborhood. The only signs of life came from the flutter of curtains as people peeked out. Some had broken windows. Others were missing doors. As he passed the smoldering remains of another home, the stench of rotting corpses violated his lungs.

He picked up his pace, jogging past more homes until he reached the intersection of a main road. Ten yards down on the right, several people carrying baseball bats entered the shattered glass doors of a twenty-four-hour sandwich shop. Next to it, an electronics store sat empty. Several broken televisions lay scattered in pieces across the parking lot.

As he continued through the city, he passed another group of people standing around a barbecue in someone's driveway. A woman in a tattered tropical patterned muumuu stirred a pot of pinto beans. She glared as he passed. Several men turned to track Luke's progression. He hurried on, not wanting to start trouble over a meager meal. He still had several energy bars and two bottles of water in his pack, so he wouldn't have to worry about food until tomorrow.

On the next block, a group of elderly people lay sprawled across a front porch. Flies swarmed their bodies. He gagged and pulled his shirt up to cover his nose. He'd expected things to be bad, but this…this looked like Baghdad circa 1991. For a moment, he was right back in the heat of battle. Shells exploding all around him. The blast of anti-aircraft fire arcing through the sky.

He staggered along the sidewalk, shaking his head

to clear the images. He didn't go back to that place often, but when he did, his whole body shook as if he was still under fire. As his vision narrowed, he sucked in a breath and held it. He released it as a long, audible whoosh. His fists unclenched, his vision returned, and the spectral gunshots vanished, only to be replaced by the real thing.

A burst of automatic gunfire cut through the silence. Luke whipped out his gun and jogged to the nearest house to take cover.

A second blast of gunshots came from one block over. Several men sporting blue bandanas retreated onto the far end of the street. Luke sank back into the shadows. With any luck, they'd pass him by without a glance. He didn't shy away from danger, but ammo was precious and he couldn't afford to waste a single shot.

The men ran down the street. In addition to baggy jeans, they wore bright white tennis shoes. Clearly brand new. Probably stolen.

Several men were shirtless. "MS 13" tattoos in an Old English font covered their chests. Gangbangers. Members of Mara Salvatrucha, an international street gang that originated in LA in the 1980s. The "13" meant they were aligned with the Mexican Mafia—not people he wanted to fuck with. One of his old SEAL buddies had done some deep cover work with the Riverside PD gang unit. He almost didn't live to testify against them.

As the men jogged past his hiding place on a porch, the youngest of the group turned and looked right at Luke. A cold fissure of fear jolted down his spine. The gangbanger lifted a finger to his neck then sliced it across as if he were slitting his throat.

Luke got the message loud and clear. After the men disappeared around the corner, he checked to make sure whoever they'd been shooting at wasn't in pursuit. He couldn't risk getting caught in the crossfire.

With the road clear in both directions, he ran to the corner and peeked around it. The gang had moved on to the next block. He headed in the opposite direction toward an industrial area. It would be less populated and presumably safer.

And for a while it was.

The hair on the back of his neck prickled. Instead of turning to look back, he glanced at the side mirror on a car as he walked past. He instantly recognized the blue bandanas. His heart thudded as adrenaline flooded his system.

If he ran, they'd chase him, and he wasn't convinced he could outrun every member of the group. He could try to take cover and shoot at them, but he only had two magazines with seven rounds farther down the hall. Several closed doors lined the walls. He opened the first door. Inside, he found a breakroom with an intact vending machine. Tables and chairs crowded the floor. He grabbed one chair and flipped it over. He unscrewed the leg and inspected it. The solid metal center was perfect.

Before darting back into the hall, he paused and listened. Eerie silence greeted him. He considered waiting in the room. Maybe they were gone. If they were lazy enough, maybe they'd given up after failing to locate him on the ground floor.

But was waiting worth the risk? If they did breach the second floor, he'd be a sitting duck. No, it was always better to take action than to wait around and hope for the best. In a world filled with lawless thugs, he had to stay on the offensive as much as possible. Maintaining a defensive position could get him killed if they trapped him. They certainly outgunned him in terms of ammo, a situation he'd have to rectify sooner than later.

He exited the room. As he walked down the hall, he mentally planned his escape. Get into the elevator shaft, slide down the cables, get into the elevator, then get the hell out of the warehouse. It would all come down to timing. If he made too much noise opening the doors, he'd be dead. If he pried open the doors on the ground floor too soon—dead.

When he reached the elevator, he heard the first set of steps coming up the stairs. With little time to waste, he used the metal table leg to pry open the elevator doors. A gaping void greeted him. He kicked himself for forgetting to grab a flashlight. But before he could reach for one, footsteps sounded on the stairs.

With only seconds to spare, he leapt into the elevator shaft and grabbed a thick cable. The doors slid closed. Hand under hand, he descended until his feet touched the top of the freight elevator. He dropped to his knees and felt around the top of the elevator, trying to locate a lock or latch.

His fingers found a raised handle. He cracked it and slowly opened the roof. When the unoiled hinges squeaked, he froze for a second before continuing to flip it over. He lowered himself into the elevator, leaving the roof open in case he needed to make a hasty retreat.

Stale cigarette smoke clung to the padded walls. Suffocating air crushed his lungs. The hot, airless coffin closed in on every side. Absolute darkness set his imagination on fire. Although he knew he was alone in the elevator, every terrifying horror film he'd ever watched flashed through his mind. He half-expected to hear a demonic child's laughter, or feel the brush of ghostly fingers down his spine.

Hysteria edged out reason. He set the table leg on the floor and took a step forward. He didn't know which side held the door. As he felt along the warm metal, his desperation increased. He fumbled across two walls before finding the control panel. In his haste, he brushed against a button. A shrill ring blasted through the elevator.

Shit! The emergency alarm must have a battery backup.

He sprang into action, tearing open the doors with the chair leg. As he burst into the hall, light from a nearby window blinded him. He squinted and ran toward an emergency exit door.

On the second floor, men shouted and rushed back to the stairs. Their shoes pounded on the metal as they raced toward the first floor. One man reached the bottom and immediately opened fire. A bullet ricocheted off the wall to his right. Another hit to his left.

Just steps from the door, a sudden, searing pain burned across his thigh. He stumbled but managed to reach the door while the thug reloaded. Luke shoved through the exit door and ran into an alleyway. He turned a corner and kept running.

After a series of zigzags, his lungs burned. A side stitch stole his breath. He had to slow down, but not yet. Not until he was sure they weren't behind him.

He skated around a dumpster and ran across a six-lane road. When he reached the other side, he risked a glance back. No one pursued him. He'd lost them somewhere in the industrial maze. Or so he hoped.

Instead of waiting around to find out, he disappeared behind a dry-cleaning store. He tested the back door. Locked.

He continued down the alley. When he emerged on the other side, he spotted a library. They'd never expect to find him there.

Seconds later, he tried the front door of the library. Locked. He circled around back and found that door locked too. He grabbed a large rock off the ground and used it to smash a hole in the window next to the back door. He pounded the glass out of the window seal. After tossing his bag inside, he vaulted into the library.

With his gun at the ready, he shouldered his bag and began to sweep the aisles. Towering shelves stuffed with books blocked his line of sight. He couldn't see into the next aisle, so he proceeded with extreme caution. Each unexplored row kicked his heartbeat up another notch. His thigh burned, but he ignored the pain.

The library was comprised of five rooms. After clearing the main bookshelf area, he checked the first

2

Liz raised a pair of night vision binoculars to her eyes. As she crept through the forest several hundred yards from her cabin, she scanned for threats. Although she didn't expect anyone from the preacher's compound to venture onto her property, she couldn't leave her family's safety to chance. Until Luke returned home, she was responsible for their kids, Sierra and Kyle.

The branches of gnarled oaks reached out to block her path in several places. She tried to memorize every step so she wouldn't have to use the binoculars, but the area was too big. Fortunately the first rays of sunlight brightened the horizon.

She hung the binoculars around her neck. As she crossed the creek that cut through her property, she squinted at the ground. So far, she hadn't spotted any tracks, but she had to remain vigilant.

A few days earlier, she'd caught several men from a nearby church trespassing on her property. She'd been forced to shoot and kill one of them when he'd attempted to infiltrate her home. She'd confronted their preacher, Elijah, in front of the entire congregation of about forty people. Although he'd denied knowing anything about the men on her land, she didn't believe him.

Since she didn't trust him, she'd outlined a series of perimeter sweeps. She'd already caught several people from the preacher's compound stealing water from the stream. Their land began over the next ridge, and she intended to make sure they stayed on it.

The sky turned indigo, then golden fire danced across the clouds. She shivered. Over the last two days, the temperature had dropped several degrees. October weather in Southern California was unpredictable at best. It could be one hundred degrees one day, and seventy the next. A lot of it depended on the Santa Ana winds. If they were blowing, it would be warmer. Fortunately they'd stopped, which in turn significantly reduced the risk of wild fires.

She walked across an acorn-covered trail. A pale shaft of sunlight spotlighted a broken twig. She stopped, bent over and picked it up. She'd never done any kind of animal tracking, but she'd cleared the path the previous day. This had to be fresh.

Three yards away, a broken twig lay on the ground. She dropped the one in her hand and headed over to the second one. A faint shoe impression in the dirt confirmed her suspicion. They'd been on her property again. To confirm it, she followed the tracks over the hill into the next canyon. They ended at the edge of the forest, a stone's throw from the preacher's compound.

She hid in the shadow of a great oak and watched the men and women of the congregation. Although they appeared to be a perfectly normal community from the outside, something wasn't right. She'd spent the last several days spying on them. Elijah seemed to control every aspect of their day. The group was too regimented, too organized, and too homogenized, like something out of a dystopian society.

If only she could talk to some of them away from Elijah's watchful eyes. Maybe things weren't as perfect as they seemed. Ultimately, she couldn't have cared less what they did as long as they stayed away from her and her kids.

As she turned to hike back toward the cabin, a branch snapped in the distance. She froze and scanned the trees. A shiver slithered down her spine.

Someone was out there, watching. She could feel their eyes on her. Invasive. Penetrating.

She stood taller and thrust back her shoulders. Her hands rested lightly on the shotgun she'd strapped across her chest in a two-point sling. Whoever was out there wasn't going to intimidate her. She wouldn't let them.

After standing her ground for several minutes, she cautiously picked a path through the woods, careful to avoid stepping on any twigs. It couldn't hurt to be extra cautious. If anything happened to her, Sierra and Kyle would be left to fend for themselves. Kyle was only thirteen, far too young to be on his own. And Sierra…

Liz shook her head. They were in this mess with the preacher's group because of her daughter. For a nineteen-year-old, she didn't seem to have a lick of common sense. Maybe Liz had been too soft on her daughter. Maybe she should have taken a harder line. Maybe she shouldn't have tried to shelter her so much. She'd tried to give her kids everything she hadn't had while growing up, but at what cost?

Hopefully Sierra had learned a valuable lesson about safety. They weren't in the regular world anymore. They'd barely escaped the post-bombing chaos. Within hours of the first nuke, riots and shootings had overwhelmed the city. The cabin was

to come by later, Sandy's been baking biscuits. I keep telling her we need to conserve gas, but she says she's too bored to sit around and knit all day. Although..." he glanced at the sky. "With the way the weather's going, I might need an extra sweater or two."

"It seems early for it to be this cold."

"You can never tell when summer will be over in So Cal. I miss being able to hop online to check the Weather Channel. Sandy used to watch it all the time. I used to hate sitting through endless updates on hurricanes on the other side of the US just so I could catch the local weather. Now I'd give anything to be so bored."

"I hear you."

"Anyway, come over in a few hours. If you can bring a side dish or two, Sandy's cooking up one of the roasts from the freezer. We're eating the fresh meat before we break into the canned stuff. I don't want to keep wasting gas on the generator to keep the freezer running. We're cycling it on and off, but it's still guzzling gas faster than I'd like."

"Sounds good. The best I can do is canned green beans and corn. We don't have a separate freezer at the cabin."

"That works. I'll let her know. We'd be happy to have some company."

"Before you go, have you seen anyone wandering

around your property?" she asked.

"I haven't really been looking."

"You might want to check on your way back. Make sure no one's been poking around."

"I'll take a look. See you later."

As he bent down to scoop water into the buckets, she turned toward her cabin. When she reached the grassy clearing in front of the cabin, Justice, her one-year-old golden retriever, came barreling down the front steps. Kyle raced behind him.

"Hey, Mom!"

"Are you ready for patrol?"

"Yep. I've got my rifle and Justice is coming with me." He turned to the dog and ruffled his fur. "Aren't you?"

"Woof!"

"Be careful. Remember, don't engage anyone. Don't shoot. You're only out there to observe. If you see anything suspicious, make note of the area and come tell me. Okay?"

"Got it."

"I'm counting on you to stay safe."

"We will."

As Kyle and Justice headed into the forest, she rubbed her temples. She hated sending him out on patrol, but with only her and Sierra, they couldn't possibly take twelve-hour shifts. As soon as Luke got home, things would change. Until then, she'd have to make due. Unless…

What if she could pull Edwin and Sandy into the group? They lived close enough that they wouldn't have to expand their perimeter walk by very much. Everyone would enjoy shorter shifts too. Having two more adults to help shoulder the duty would take a huge weight off her shoulders. But would they be willing to do it? They hadn't had any trouble with Elijah, so they really didn't have any incentive to help, but it couldn't hurt to ask. Worst case scenario, they'd say no, and she'd be right back where she started. But if they said yes, then she'd get a few extra hours of sleep each day. It was worth a shot.

Liz waited until everyone's bellies were filled with Sandy's succulent pot roast before broaching the subject of sharing watch duties. As Kyle and Sierra cleared the dishes, Liz leaned back against the log cabin wall and sighed.

"I haven't eaten that well in weeks."

"I'm glad you came over," Sandy said. "I was afraid I'd have to eat all of those biscuits myself."

"Can we take some home?" Kyle asked.

"Kyle!" Liz shook her head. "We can't take any

more food from you. We don't know how long the power outage is going to last."

"It's okay," Sandy said. "I've got enough flour and baking powder stored up to feed an army. Anytime you need anything, come on over."

"I might take up you on that," Liz said. She turned toward Edwin, who sat at the head of the table. "Did you have a chance to look around?"

"Yeah." His gaze darted to his wife before returning to Liz. "I found tracks near the shed."

"What kind of tracks?" Sandy asked.

"Boot prints."

"Who'd be interested in our shed? We don't have anything valuable back there."

"We've got the fuel for the generator."

"Someone would have to cart it off in a wheelbarrow or something," Sandy said. "I know most of the people in the canyon. I can't see any of them stealing from us."

"Other people might not be as well supplied," Liz said. "I've been thinking, maybe we should work together to keep watch over both of our properties. Since they butt up against each other on one side, it won't be very hard."

When Edwin and Sandy glanced at each other, Liz frowned. Sandy pressed her lips together. Edwin shifted in his chair.

think about it."

"I doubt you'll have any problem with them," Sandy said. "They've always been really nice to us. We even swap flour for sugar sometimes."

"They're probably very nice," Liz said. "But given the trouble we had recently, I don't know if I'm ready to meet another group."

"Understandable," Sandy said. "Let us know what you decide. In the meantime, we won't mention anything to them. We wouldn't want them showing up unannounced."

"Thank you."

"Is there anything for dessert?" Kyle asked.

"Dishes are done," Sierra said.

"Of course I have dessert. You two are the best helpers I've ever seen," Sandy said.

Sierra smiled for the first time in days. Maybe Liz shouldn't have come down on her so hard after the incident with the preacher. At least Sierra seemed to be over the pouting phase. After finding out about her rendezvous with a boy from the church, Liz had grounded her. She wasn't allowed to leave the house other than for chores and patrol. Maybe she could finally let up a bit. Give her more freedom.

"I hope you like apple pie," Sandy said. "I had to use canned apples, but I made up for it with brown sugar."

"It smells amazing," Sierra said.

Liz felt a twinge of guilt. She'd been feeding the kids rice and beans every day, hoping to preserve the canned food until they absolutely couldn't stand rice and beans anymore. Then she'd planned on incorporating a can here and there to add variety.

Two weeks ago, they'd been able to have almost any kind of food imaginable. The proliferation of grocery stores in their neighborhood covered every type of cuisine from Mexican, to Asian, to Indian. They even had an authentic New York-style deli. What she wouldn't give for a pastrami on rye. Before the bombs, she'd taken her food options for granted. Now she would have given anything for a slice of pepperoni pizza.

As Sandy slid a piece of steaming pie in front of her, Liz inhaled the hedonistic aroma of cinnamon, nutmeg, and clove. The smell of fall. Of pumpkins and Thanksgiving. She hoped they'd be able to celebrate something this year. She held out little hope for the return of electricity if they had been hit by an EMP, but maybe they could go on some food runs into the city. Shore up their supplies. They had plenty of canned goods back at the house. She didn't need them right now, but in a few months, she may have wished she'd returned to grab all the food she could.

3

Luke jolted awake. A pitch-black room. Silence. The library. Right. He shook off the last vestige of sleep and rolled his shoulders. After groping around, he located his pack. He pulled a small flashlight out and flicked it on.

Shadows stretched across the classroom. He checked his leg. The bleeding had stopped and even though it still stung, it didn't hurt nearly as bad.

Progress. He'd take it when he could get it. The wins were few and far between, so he intended to celebrate every one of them. At this point, hope was all he had to go on. Without hope, he'd never make it home.

His stomach rumbled. After sorting through his pack, he devoured two energy bars and a Snickers. He washed it down with half of his second bottle of water before screwing the cap back on. Until he found a new water source, he couldn't finish it off.

As he climbed to his feet, pain shot down his leg. He growled and shook it off. Bad idea. Flashes of white-hot fire sizzled along his nerves. He sighed and waited until the worst of it passed before attempting to take a step. He'd wanted to avoid taking any painkillers since he had such a limited supply to begin with, but he needed to keep moving.

After popping two aspirin, he hobbled to the door. He listened for movement outside. Nothing. Even though he doubted he'd have to contend with anyone in the library, he remained cautious as he entered the hall. He backtracked to the office with the desk. Sometimes people kept snacks in their offices.

Normally he'd never steal from someone, but these weren't normal times. If the librarian had needed extra food, she would have come back by now. She either lived too far away, had plenty of preps at home, or she was already dead.

He sat in the chair behind the desk and began opening drawers. The first two didn't hold anything of interest. He opened the third drawer and smiled. An unopened snack pack of tuna and crackers sat next to a sleeve of butter cookies. He tore into the

contained maps of various countries. The third row housed road maps of the surrounding area. He pulled out a map of the Inland Empire. With all the running he'd been doing, he had no idea where he was. He headed to the front of the building and checked the concrete sign. Rialto Public Library.

He whipped open a map and laid it out on the checkout desk. Of course the map didn't list libraries, so he needed the address. He found it on a business card.

As he ran his finger across the map, he searched for First Street. He found it and followed the line to the 200 block. Damn. He'd gotten way off course. He was five miles west of Highway 215. He'd been using it as a guide until the gang had chased him.

He began to draw various routes through the city. South Riverside Street crossed the Santa Ana River about five miles to the south. That could work, then he could use the trees around the river as cover. Although, it was hard to tell from the map whether or not the river would flow above ground. Some rivers were piped through cities underground. In that case, it wouldn't help him. But he wouldn't know until he reached it.

As he looked for alternative routes, he noticed hash marks near downtown Rialto. Train tracks? He leaned down and squinted at the map. The Rialto

Train Station was two blocks away. Finally, a break. Talk about getting lucky. He almost couldn't believe it. The train tracks would be a much better option. It wasn't without risks, but train tracks usually ran behind buildings. Unless someone else had the same idea, he could end up with the tracks all to himself.

After folding up that map, he rifled through the next rack down. Utility maps. These could come in handy. He set aside all of the electrical grid maps. They were useless now. But the storm drain lines, those could be beneficial if he needed to plot a route underground. If he kept running into more problems on the surface, going below ground might be a good option. He added that map to the pile.

Outside, the last rays of sunshine faded. Still racked with pain, he decided to spend the night in the library.

Back inside the classroom, he settled in for the night. The muted crack of gunfire carried through the walls. Although he doubted anyone would think to check the library for anything useful, they might see the broken glass at the back door and decide to investigate.

He lifted his pistol and hit the mag release. After grabbing the full mag from his pack, he slammed it into the gun. He cocked and locked it before laying it at his side.

The door could be a problem. No lock. If anyone came in shooting, he was a dead man, but most people were lazy. If he pushed a few tables up against the door, they might think it was locked. He flipped three tables on their sides and shoved them up against the door. He added several chairs to the pile. It might not be enough to keep people out, but at least it would give him a few seconds' warning. Hopefully it would be enough.

LUKE WOKE at dawn to a dull throbbing in his thigh. He sat up to check the wound. After peeling the gauze away, he squeezed the wound to check for puss. A thin trickle of blood oozed out. Not bad. He wouldn't be healed before he reached home, but that didn't matter. Liz wouldn't care as long as he made it home in one piece.

He used the last of the water in his second bottle to clean the wound, then reapplied a fresh layer of antibiotic ointment. He covered the wound with gauze and repacked his bag. When he tried to clear his throat, his tongue stuck to the roof of his mouth. He needed to locate water as soon as possible. Dehydration would take him down faster than almost anything else, so until he got home, it would have to be his top priority.

The pile of tables and chairs still blocked the door to the classroom. Luke untangled the mass of furniture. Before opening the door, he stopped to listen for any movement outside. The library was as silent as a mausoleum.

He cracked open the door and peeked out into an empty hallway. Good, at least he wouldn't have to shoot his way out.

Before leaving the library, he checked the other rooms. He didn't find any water, so he headed out the rear entrance.

Outside, a gray haze drifted across the sky. It couldn't be smog since cars weren't running, but it could be from the fires. The temperature had dropped about ten degrees compared to the previous day. An analog thermometer on the outside of the building displayed seventy-eight degrees. Not too hot, but not cool by any means.

He walked around the outside of the building until he found a hose bib sticking out of the wall. It was attached to a small, two-inch pipe about as big around as his thumb. The water valve could potentially give him access to all the water he could ever want, provided water flowed through the line.

After pulling a four-way steel sillcock key wrench

The glass doors out front remained intact. Looting a police station would be idiotic, but desperate overrode reason in a disaster scenario. This certainly qualified as one.

A sign had been taped to the glass from inside.

No services. Closed until further notice.

He cupped his hands against the glass and peered inside. The building was empty but for a few desks and some chairs. His fantasy of being able to use a satellite phone to call Liz evaporated. They probably wouldn't have let him use it anyway if they'd had one. Oh well. Onward.

Silence amplified the sound of his footsteps. He scanned both sides of the road as well as the street. It was surreal. No one was in sight. It was as if he was the last man on earth. He knew it wasn't true, but the absolute stillness unnerved him. He hadn't realized how much background noise he'd encountered in everyday life. Usually airplanes buzzed overhead. Car horns honked and tires screeched. Some drivers yelled at each other, while others blasted music. Without all of the added stimulation, he was able to be extra alert to sounds he never would have heard before the bombs dropped.

A raven cawed from its perch atop a light pole. It glared at him with beady black eyes. God, he hated birds. He'd been attacked by one on his parents' farm when he was a kid. Damn bird had tried to peck the hair out of his head to use it in its nest.

As he continued down the road, a gust of wind propelled a fast food wrapper past his feet. The crumpled wrapper scraped against the gravel as it rolled.

Halfway up a flag pole, an American flag cracked in the wind. He paused, his heart full of love for his country. Until now he'd been completely obsessed with the fate of his family. But there were so many families out there just like his. Families who hadn't prepared for war. Families who were starving, defenseless, and headed toward certain death.

All the warning signs had been in the news for months. Political instability, trade wars, and posturing between various countries had finally reached a flash point. It didn't matter who had struck first. Maybe the whole world was at war. Maybe the president had authorized the launch of nuclear weapons and other countries had retaliated.

As he turned onto the train tracks, he sighed and ran a hand through his hair. He'd spent the last few years trying to prepare his family, not just for war, but for anything that might come up. If he'd lost his job, they would have been okay. He had several months' worth of food stocked up between the house and the cabin. If the San Andreas Fault had ruptured causing "The Big One," he would have been ready. A few years ago, nuclear war hadn't even been within the realm of possibility, at least in his mind. But now, he was damn glad he'd prepared. Now they'd have a fighting chance.

Lost in his thoughts, he almost didn't hear the second set of footsteps on the track. Thirty yards behind, the person kept pace with Luke. A chain link fence with razor wire lined the right side of the tracks. He wouldn't even attempt to climb over it. One wrong move and he'd get tangled up and sliced and diced by the razors.

To his left, several warehouses lined the tracks. A razorless chain link fence separated him from the protection of the buildings, but he could be up and over them in seconds.

As he debated what to do, he kept walking. Same pace, same level of relaxation in his posture. If he tensed up, the other person would know he'd been spotted. Whoever it was hadn't made a move to either draw closer, or draw down on him.

With the element of surprise on his side, he took several long, slow breaths to fully oxygenate his blood. He counted to three before sprinting toward the fence. Up and over in seconds, he dashed across a weed-choked path before hiding behind the edge of the warehouse.

The fence rattled as the other man climbed it.

Luke peered around the corner. The other guy was about five foot ten. A baseball hat partially obscured his face, but based on the way he lumbered across the path, he had to be in his forties. A classic beer belly rose up from underneath a sweat-stained gray T-shirt. He wore black cotton shorts crusted with dirt.

Luke eased back into the shadows. He didn't make his move until the man turned the corner.

He grabbed the man by the throat, spun his back to the wall, and pointed his gun at the man's forehead. "Who the fuck are you and why are you following me?"

"Because I have more experience with people. I can sense if something's not right."

"I can sense that too. I knew something wasn't right with Elijah."

"And yet you continued to go over there," Liz said.

"They had cookies with real sugar."

"Not a valid excuse."

"Fine. But I'm not an idiot."

"People from the preacher's group *shot* at us," Liz said through clenched teeth. "Your continued interaction with them was *not* a case of good judgment."

Sierra huffed and folded her arms over her chest.

"Until you learn to read people for who they really are, you need to stay away from them."

"How can I learn to read people if I never talk to anyone but you and Kyle?" Sierra asked.

"You can learn later. Right now I need you to take watch. I'm going over to the Wrights. I should be back in a few hours. If anything happens, I'll be at the house closest to Santiago Canyon Road."

"Whatever." Sierra stood and dumped her coffee in the sink.

"Don't waste food," Liz said.

"We've got plenty of coffee. Besides, I ran a second pot of water through it like you told me to do. It's weak as hell and nasty, but I guess it's still coffee."

"In a few months we might not have any coffee left. We need to stretch it out as much as we can."

"I wish the world would either end, or not end. Being in limbo sucks," Sierra said.

Liz silently agreed.

"Take care of your brother. I'll be back soon."

"You're not going to take a nap first?"

"No. If this group is worth joining, then I'll be able to sleep a lot more."

"That would be nice," Sierra said, as if she didn't already sleep more than her fair share.

"I found footprints out by the stream. When you head out there, be extra vigilant."

"I will."

"Remember, don't talk to anyone. Run home and lock the door if you see anyone."

"Can't I just shoot them instead? They'd be on our property."

"No! I'm getting sick of your attitude. This isn't a big joke. Someone died already."

"I know." Sierra averted her gaze.

"We're in the middle of a disaster worse than anything in human history. We don't know when it will end. We don't know *if* it will end. It's time you start taking this seriously. Every choice we make has long-term consequences now. Something that might seem inconsequential today could have horrible repercussions down the line."

"I know."

"I don't think you do," Liz said. "If you're not careful, you could be killed. Your brother could be killed. You can't take risks, not now."

"Fine. I won't."

"Okay." Liz softened her tone. "I'm not mad at you, I'm trying to protect you. Your dad will be home in a few days, and if I can make a deal with the other people living in the canyon, then things will get better for us. Hang in there."

"I should get going."

Sierra grabbed a rifle from its resting place near the door. She pushed back the corner of the curtains to check outside, just like Liz had taught her to do. After removing the two by four barricade, she pushed open the door and stepped onto the porch.

Liz stood and crossed to the window. As she watched her daughter disappear into the woods, she couldn't shake the ever-present cloak of dread. Although she hadn't encountered the preacher directly, he was out there. She could feel it.

After feeding Justice and making breakfast for Kyle, she headed up to the Wrights' house. Edwin sat on a rocking chair on their front porch. Sandy waved from the kitchen window.

"You're up early," Edwin said.

"Just finished my shift."

"Any new tracks?"

"Nothing since yesterday. If the offer's still good, I'd like to meet the other people in your watch group."

"Great. We can walk over there after breakfast. Did you already eat?"

"Yes."

"Any biscuits?"

"No flour. I really wish I had packed as much flour as I did rice and beans," she said.

"We'll stuff you full of biscuits then be on our way."

"Sounds good."

"Pull up a chair. Sandy will be out in a minute. How are things with the kids?"

She sighed. Although she didn't want to burden anyone with her problems, it would be nice to talk to another adult about Sierra.

"My daughter and I have been at each other's throats since running into the preacher. I don't understand how she ended up so…"

"Naïve?"

"I hate to say it, but yes."

"She's still a kid."

"She's nineteen."

"Doesn't matter. Kids are different these days.

stream. Still pissed from the conversation she'd had with her mom, she needed a way to blow off steam. Tossing rocks seemed like the only option. Part of her wished she'd stayed in her dorm room at UC Irvine. Ever since she'd arrived at the cabin, her mom had been on her. Do the dishes. Sweep the cabin. Wash the laundry. Nothing was ever good enough for her.

After walking the perimeter twice, Sierra stopped at the stream to wash the dust off her legs. She hiked up her shorts and splashed water on her knees. As it trickled down her skin, goosebumps formed. A cloudless gray sky covered the forest. Within an hour or two of sunrise, the sun disappeared behind a blanket of haze. She'd never seen anything so strange. Normally the marine layer would have burned off hours ago. It was almost as if there was smoke in the sky. She sniffed the air. It didn't smell smoky.

A branch snapped across the stream. Her head snapped up. She peered into the forest. In the distance, a figure walked along the trail. She stepped behind an oak and shouldered her rifle, keeping it trained on the person.

Her mom had told her to run home if she spotted anyone, but maybe it was Adam. No one would ever know if she only stayed a few extra seconds to check. She'd been dying to see him. She hadn't had a chance to talk to him since her mother had confronted the preacher several days earlier. Hopefully he wasn't in trouble too.

When Adam stepped into the clearing near the stream, she dropped the gun to her side. Her heart thumped as he drew closer. With shaggy brown surfer hair, a deep tan, and bright blue eyes, he was the epitome of hot. They were the same age, which made things so much easier. He understood her in a way her mom never could.

"Hey!" she called.

"You scared the crap out of me," Adam said. "I didn't see you standing over there."

"Sorry. I wasn't sure if it was you or someone else."

"Were you waiting for someone else?"

"No."

"What are you doing out here with a gun?" he asked.

"I'm..." She hesitated. She wasn't supposed to tell anyone about their security measures, but it was Adam. Not some weird stranger. Although she didn't know him very well, he seemed cool. "I was out on patrol."

"Patrol? Why?"

"Mom's worried about Elijah. She thinks he's going to come back and try to take the cabin from us."

"She might be right," he said.

"What?"

"That's why I'm out here. I was looking for you so I could warn you."

"Did Elijah say something?"

"I was behind the church by this shed they keep locked all the time. I was trying to look inside to see what's in there. No one's supposed to go behind the church."

"But you were curious anyway."

"Yep. Can you blame me?"

"No. I'd try to check it out too."

"Exactly."

"Did you see anything?"

"No, but while I was back there, I overheard Elijah and Turner talking about your mom."

"What did they say?"

"They've been watching your house."

"That's creepy."

"Seriously."

"Why are they watching us?"

"Elijah told Turner he's worried about your mom's influence over his flock. It's so strange that he keeps calling us his flock. Like we're sheep or something."

"You guys follow him around a lot."

"Only because he was in the most obvious leadership position."

"What about your dad?" she asked.

"I don't have one."

"Everyone has a dad."

"Mine died."

"I'm sorry."

"It was a long time ago."

"Have you heard any more news about the bombs?" she asked.

"No. I just assume whoever is bombing us is trying to wipe democracy off the face of the planet or something. There are so many crazy-ass dictators out there. It could be any of them. Russia. China. North Korea."

"We'll find out eventually," she said with conviction. "Anyway, what else did Elijah say about us?"

"He said for now he just wants Turner to keep an eye on the house. They're trying to figure out who lives there. They know about you, your mom, and your brother, but they haven't spotted your dad yet."

"That's because—" She stopped short. How much did she really trust Adam? What if Elijah had sent him to spy on her? To get information about her family? Until she knew for sure, she wouldn't reveal the truth about her dad. "He's been on patrol a lot too."

"Where does he patrol?"

Her eyebrows crinkled together. Why was he

find out more and warn you if they're planning something. Do you come to the stream a lot?"

"I've got morning shift. I'm usually here an hour after sunrise."

"Can I come see you again?" he asked.

"As long as you keep it a secret. My mom would kick my ass if she knew we were meeting."

"I'm not sure what my mom would do, but Elijah would be pissed. I won't tell anyone."

"Good."

He gave her hand a squeeze before releasing it. She bit the edge of her lip and smiled. As he walked back toward the trail, her gaze dropped to his butt. So cute. At least she had something to look forward to now.

She resumed patrol, skirting the edge of the stream for a half mile before turning back toward the house. She hadn't really violated any of her mom's rules. Adam wasn't a stranger, and her mom had no right to dictate who she could and couldn't talk to. She'd still be careful not to reveal her dad's whereabouts to Adam, just in case. But she was pretty sure she could trust him.

5

Liz brushed dirt stains from her shirt as she and Edwin approached the other neighbor's house. She hadn't thought to take a shower before heading over. Maybe it wouldn't be a big deal. Immaculate hygiene belonged to the old world, for now. Eventually things would return to normal, but until then, people couldn't be too upset about a little extra dirt.

Edwin headed up the porch steps and knocked on the front door. For a group seemingly concerned about security, it seemed odd that they'd let Edwin bring a stranger over. Maybe he'd already talked to them late last night.

The door swung open and a woman with stripes of silver in her hair walked out. She had pinched features and a beak-like hooked nose. A pair of glasses were perched on the end of it. She pushed them up and regarded Liz with a hawk-like gaze.

"So you're the woman from up the road. The one with the trouble?" she asked.

"Irene, this is Liz," Edwin said.

"It's nice to meet you," Liz said. "Edwin's told me all about you."

"Has he?"

Liz's gaze bounced between them. What exactly had Edwin told her? This wasn't the warm welcome she'd anticipated. Maybe she needed to reset her expectations.

"Edwin told us you've been having trouble with the church the next canyon over," Irene said. "He said someone got shot and killed."

"A group of men trespassed on my property. They had guns, so I considered them a threat. The guy I shot was less than ten yards from my house. I have every right."

"No one's saying you didn't," Edwin said. "Is Harvey home?"

"He's out back taking care of the goats."

"You have goats?" Liz asked. They weren't in farm country, so the presence of any kind of livestock other than horses was surprising.

"Milk goats."

"I'd love to see them," Liz said.

"All right then, I guess it wouldn't hurt."

As Irene led them around the side of the house into the backyard, Liz shot a questioning look at Edwin. He shrugged his shoulders as if he wasn't sure what to make of Irene's attitude. Was she always like this, or was she simply against bringing another person into the group?

Harvey sat on a stool just inside a small red barn. He milked a goat into a silver bucket. As they approached, he turned to greet them.

"Hello! You caught me in the middle of milking, but if you don't mind it, you're welcome to watch while we talk."

"How's old Bessie doing?" Edwin asked.

"She's as ornery as a peacock in heat today."

"What do you do with all the milk?" Liz asked.

"Mostly turn it into goat cheese, but we keep some for drinking."

"Are you almost done?" Irene asked. "I want to get back to the house. I've got laundry to do."

"I'll be done in about five minutes. I'll bring it up. You can head in if you want," Harvey said.

She turned without a word and walked back to the house.

"She's in a foul mood," Harvey said as soon as she was out of earshot. "She gets like that when the

"We'll see him coming long before he sees us," Harvey said. "We've got lookouts on the hills."

"Really?" Liz lifted her hand to shade her eyes. As she scanned the surrounding landscape, light glinted off something on the highest hill. Probably binoculars or a gun. "Your people aren't concealed very well."

"Owen's on watch right now. The boy doesn't have more than two cents to rub together in his head. I think he smoked too much pot before the bombs dropped. Fried his brain cells. I keep telling him to stay behind a bush, but he insists on plopping down on his ass wherever he damn well pleases."

"That's unfortunate," Liz said, keeping her own assessment to herself. If she'd voiced her true opinion, it might serve to burn bridges before she'd even built any.

"I've been thinking about your situation and here's where I'm at. We'll take you on a trial basis. After thirty days, if everything's going well, we'll officially welcome you to the group. Based on where you live, we're going to have to extend our perimeter out to the edge of your property. That means you might catch us walking around out there while on patrol. Now, we can't have you shooting us, so I'd want you to meet everyone first so we can get this set up."

"When do you typically meet?" she asked.

"Once a day, usually at night. Sometimes we eat dinner together, but most of the time we just do a quick, thirty-minute check-in right before sunset. We really haven't had much to report, but if we're going to be out on your property, we might have more to discuss."

"I'm pretty sure the preacher's men are wandering onto my property near the stream."

"Are they there to take water?" Harvey asked.

"Not as far as I can tell. I think they're watching us."

"Maybe if they know there's more people watching out for you, they'll back off."

"That's what I'm hoping. I'd really appreciate all the help I can get," she said.

"We'll see what we can do. Why don't you come by tonight, right before sunset. I'll introduce you to the group and see what everyone thinks about bringing your family in on a trial basis. This wouldn't be a done deal until they've all had a chance to meet you."

"I understand."

"I'd better get this pail in there before it starts to sour. See you tonight."

As Harvey carried the pail into the house, Liz and Edwin circled around to the road in front. They walked up the road toward Edwin's house.

"So, what did you think?" Edwin asked.

"It sounds promising."

"I don't think anyone's going to have a problem bringing you in. He's just being cautious."

"As he should be. It shows consideration for the group."

After saying goodbye to him, Liz strolled back toward the cabin. Along the way, she checked the tripwire. She and Kyle had spent hours tying bells to fishing line before stringing it between trees. It wasn't the most high-tech option, but in a post-electric world, it worked as well as anything. Whether or not it would be enough to warn them remained to be seen, but for now, it was better than nothing.

AN HOUR BEFORE SUNSET, Liz kissed the kids goodbye before heading over to Edwin and Sandy's house. They showed her the way to the group's meeting place, a fire pit behind one of the other cabins. Apprehension tingled in her gut. Harvey and Irene stood across the fire from her. They held mason jars full of clear liquid. Water? Vodka? She couldn't tell without being close enough to smell it.

"Would you like a drink?" a man asked.

She turned to find a middle-aged man with salt and pepper hair standing behind her. He had the uptight manor of a nobleman, or a literature professor. If his nose was any farther in the air, he could use it as a barometer. Did it twitch when a storm was on its way?

"I'll have whatever they're having," she said.

"One vodka tonic, coming up."

She smiled until he turned his back, then wrinkled her nose. Yuck! She hated tonic water. Maybe she should have asked for plain water instead.

A pair of gorgeous twin girls walked up from the road. They looked slightly older than Sierra. Probably twenty-one or twenty-two. They wore matching jeans with light pink T-shirts. Even their ponytails swung in tandem.

"I'm Carla," the one on the right said as she held out a hand. After Liz shook it, Carla gestured toward her sister. "This is Noelle. We're twins."

"Obviously," Noelle said with a laugh. "She does that."

"What?" Carla asked.

"Likes to state the obvious."

Noelle snorted hard enough to whip her ponytail to one side.

"It's nice to meet you," Liz said, noting the faint mole on Carla's cheek. She tried to memorize which twin had the mole and which didn't, but would prob-

"Right now we're a close-knit community. We haven't had any problems so far. We all work well together, don't we?"

Several heads nodded.

"We don't need to bring new members into the fold. Sure, we have to share a lot of shifts to make sure someone's watching 24/7, but overall, we've got this." Jamie flashed a thousand-watt smile.

"Does anyone else have anything to say?" Harvey asked.

"I do." Irene stood. "If we allow her into the community, how do we know she won't bring trouble with her? If the church has a problem with her, then maybe there's a good reason. Decent people don't make enemies."

"They're not decent people," Liz said. "The way he's running his congregation is cult-like. I wouldn't be surprised if I went over one day and found them all dead from drinking Kool-Aid. As long as the preacher's in charge over there, none of us are safe."

"Do you think he's going to stop with me? No. He'll kill me and my family, then come for you next. I'm the first line of defense against him, but I need your help. I can't do it all alone."

"What about your kids?" Jamie asked.

"With three people, we're on eight-hour shifts each. Mine's about ten p.m. until sunrise. Sierra's is sunrise to mid-afternoon, and Kyle's lasts until I take over again. We never see each other together anymore. It's…" She stopped, not wanting to reveal that their current schedule was tearing her family apart.

"I see your point," Irene said. "She's right. If the preacher decides to come for our supplies, what's to stop him?"

"I promise you I'll do everything in my power to make sure you never have to deal with him. I'll contribute to the community in whatever way you see fit. The only thing I ask in return is a break from eight-hour shifts."

"The power's been out for days," Harvey said. "We don't know how long it's going to stay out. It could be a few days, a few weeks, or longer."

"Do you really think the power company's going to leave us without power for several weeks?" Jamie asked.

"It could be years," Liz said.

"Years?" Jamie's face contorted as if she'd swallowed a porcupine.

"If we got hit by an EMP, it's going to take years to get the power grid back up," Edwin said. "They don't keep spare parts lying around. They'd have to get one plant online to even run the manufacturing plant to make more. And even in full production mode, they can only repair a few power stations at a time. If they start on the East Coast, we could be dead last. That's why we need to band together. We could be in this for a long time."

A mixture of horrified looks and resolute silence filtered through the group.

"Does anyone else want to speak before we vote?" Harvey asked.

Everyone murmured no.

"We don't hide our votes, so if you're in favor of letting Liz and her kids into the group, say aye."

Everyone except Jamie raised their hand. Her shoulders slumped as she glanced around at the others. After several seconds, she finally raised her hand.

"Great, then it's settled," Harvey said. "Let's spend the rest of the night celebrating."

Drinks flowed. Animated conversations ensued. It was as if someone had flipped a switch. Any latent hostility evaporated on the chilly night air.

Liz stepped closer to the fire. A canopy of twinkling stars hung over the group. Other than having to deal with the preacher, surviving the apocalypse hadn't been too bad. They had plenty of food and an unlimited water source. In a few days Luke would be home, and they'd be a family again. She couldn't wait to kiss him under the stars.

6

Luke pressed the gun to the man's temple. "You'd better start talking or I'm going to start shooting."

"Wait…wait…" the man blathered. "I wasn't following you. I was walking on the tracks. Same as you."

"You were pacing me." Luke squeezed the man's throat and pushed him against the wall.

"No. No. I'm just trying to get home."

"From where?"

"Las Vegas. I was on vacation when the bombs dropped. My buddy had his bachelor party there."

"How did you get this far?"

"I walked."

"Where are your friends?"

"Then why not work together?"

"What would you bring to this partnership?" Luke asked.

"Other than my good looks?" Boyd chuckled. "Well, I may as well be a water diviner."

"Please don't tell me you walk around with a stick searching for water."

"No. No mumbo-jumbo stuff. I don't know why or how, but I seem to be able to find water in the strangest places. Let me give you an example. I was walking through the desert with my buddies. We'd run out of water a full day earlier. It was hot as hell, sun beating down on us, air as dry as a ninety-year-old snatch. But I had this feeling—walk over those hills and you'll find water. Well, I walked over those hills and—BAM! I found a spring."

"We're in the city now. It's not hard to find water here," Luke said.

"Then let me carry your pack or something. We'll be stronger together. It's not good to go it alone."

"I've done fine so far."

"Looks like you're bandaged up pretty good." Boyd pointed at Luke's leg. "You've got a bit of a limp to you already. When did it happen?"

"Yesterday."

"Knife?"

"Gunshot."

"Oh hell. How are you up and around?"

"It grazed me. Look, I'm sorry you're alone, but we're not too far from Corona. Maybe thirty miles or so. You'll be fine."

"Were you such a stubborn asshole before the bombs dropped too? Or is that a newly acquired trait?" Boyd asked.

"Good luck," Luke said as he shouldered his pack.

He headed toward the fence that stood between him and the train tracks.

"Wait! Wait!" Boyd yelled.

Luke whipped around and pointed his gun at him. "You're not coming with me. So unless you want to get shot, you'd better stay put for ten minutes. Then you can get back on the tracks. But if I so much as smell you, I'll put a round right between your eyes."

"Asshole!"

Luke narrowed his gaze. If he'd had a full pack of ammo, he would have put a bullet in his head already. Who the hell did that guy think he was? He had no weapons, no skills, and nothing to offer. He'd only slow Luke down. Sure, he felt a pang of guilt for leaving Boyd to fend for himself, but tough shit. Compassion for a stranger sat somewhere near the bottom of his list of priories in a post-apocalyptic world. And he sure as hell wasn't going to let anyone slow him down. No one's family mattered more than his own.

After jumping the fence, he headed down the tracks. Ten minutes after leaving Boyd, he turned to check to make sure he wasn't behind him. The tracks remained empty as far as he could see. Good. He didn't have time to worry about anyone else. He was already off track and needed to cover twenty miles today.

The next few miles passed in a monotonous parade. The area around the tracks left the warehouse district and morphed into residential streets. Occasionally, a person's head would appear over a fence. To stay out of the line of sight, he stuck to one side of the tracks. A brick wall separated the tracks from the homes. He stayed as close to the wall as possible. He could pull himself up and over if necessary, but for now, everything seemed peaceful.

Meat sizzled on barbecues. The smell of cooking food taunted him. It would be far too easy to hop over the fence and take whatever they were cooking. He hated to acknowledge the part of him that could imagine stealing from other people. To take food from an office desk was one thing, to take it directly from a hungry person was another.

By the time the world returned to normal, what atrocities might he commit? Would he ever give in to his darker instincts? He wouldn't go around murdering people unless provoked. But if they stood between him and food for his family, would morality take flight? He hoped to God he'd never have to find out.

A road crossing appeared in the distance. Sometimes the tracks burrowed under the roads, sometimes over them. This time the tracks disappeared into a long tunnel. He palmed his SIG. As he approached the tunnel, he passed a pile of two by four boards. Rusting nails poked up, some were covered with a glossy, reddish-brown substance. He moved closer.

Blood.

The hair on the back of his neck stood on end. He glanced at both sides of the embankment as he continued walking. Both appeared clear, but something didn't feel right. The whole setup would make the perfect choke point. He considered backtracking. Going through the houses would be risky, but at least he'd have places to run and hide.

Before he could make up his mind, the screech of metal against metal sent chills down his spine. He spun toward the sound.

Three men wearing red bandanas strolled out of the tunnel. One carried a metal fence post. Another held a brick. The third hoisted a baseball bat wrapped in barbed wire over his shoulder.

with a monstrous scream. A man swung a two by four through the air. It smashed into the thug's face, delivering a lethal blow. Blood spewed out of his mouth to spray everything within a three-foot radius. The thug crumbled to the ground. The light went from his eyes, as if someone had flicked a kill switch to end his life.

Luke sat up and wiped sweat and blood from his eyes.

"You good?" Boyd asked as he offered him a hand.

"Yeah."

"There's three more. I hope you're a good shot."

Behind him, rapid footsteps crashed through gravel. Luke grabbed the gun. He slammed the magazine home, turned, cocked the hammer, and then fired at the remaining men. He put a bullet between the first attacker's eyes. The thug tumbled forward, face planting against the outer edge of one railroad track.

The guy with the metal fence post gripped it like a javelin and hurled it through the air. Luke easily dodged it. He hit him slightly low and wide, taking his eye out with the kill shot.

"Where are the shooters?" Luke asked.

"Running away."

"Fucking cowards." Luke hit the magazine release and slammed a new magazine in.

"How much ammo do you have?"

"Seven, plus one left in the first mag." Luke pulled back the slide to load a round. "Where the hell did you come from?"

"I was following you."

"I didn't see you on the tracks."

"Up there." Boyd pointed at the wall separating the tracks from the houses. "Figured I could keep an eye on you."

"I could have handled it."

"Four to one with more coming?" Boyd laughed. "Let me guess, you're one of those bad-asses who never needs help from anyone. Am I right?"

Luke glared, but didn't respond.

"You could at least thank me," Boyd said.

"Thanks."

"So seeing as I saved your life and all, can I come with you now?"

"You're like a dog with a bone."

"Damn right. Did I mention I'm determined as shit to get home?" Boyd asked in a joking tone.

"You didn't have to. I get it. Look, I'm not slowing my pace for you."

"I've been able to keep up so far."

"Right. But don't expect me to slow down or take care of you."

"Okay, Dad."

"You're kind of a dick," Luke said.

"Gotta stir the pot once in a while. I like to keep people on their toes. So what's the plan?"

"Less talking, more walking."

"Works for me. But I'm thinking we should avoid the tunnel. The housing tract isn't too bad. I haven't run into many people. Saw a lot of burned-out houses up there."

"Lead the way," Luke said.

As much as he wanted to stay on his own, he couldn't ignore Boyd. The man had saved his life. He was annoying as shit, but not a bad guy.

Two hours later, Luke wanted to gag him. Boyd talked nonstop about anything and everything.

"…And so then I look at the blackjack dealer and I'm like—'Hit me!' You know what she does?"

"No," Luke said dryly.

"She says to me, 'Baby, I'd love to slap you right across that filthy mouth of yours, but the eye in the sky's watching and I need my job.' Hottest damn thing I ever heard."

"You're married."

"And I love my wife. Now, don't get me wrong, I like to check out the merchandise, but it doesn't mean

I'm buying. Speaking of buying stuff, I could go for some food. I finished off my last bag of chips this morning and my stomach's growling like a grizzly bear momma in spring."

"What?" Luke stopped walking.

"You know, bear moms get all protective of their cubs. Like to claw your face off if you're not careful."

"I actually know what you mean," Luke said.

"No shit. Bear get you good one time?"

"Yeah. After the bombs dropped I had to hike part of the Pacific Crest Trail. Ran into a grizzly somewhere between LA and the Cajon Pass."

"She take a swipe at you?"

"Clawed me." Luke lifted his shirt to show Boyd the still-healing marks on his back. "But I got away."

"Sounds like a hell of a story. Why don't we find some food and cop a squat for a bit?"

"Okay."

Although Luke wanted to keep walking nonstop, they needed to rest. His water was running low and Boyd had run out over an hour ago. They'd made it through several neighborhoods unharmed. The afternoon heat wasn't nearly as high as he'd expected it to be, but people seemed to have retreated into their homes anyway.

"Where should we look?" Boyd asked.

"All the obvious places will have been picked over

7

The next morning, Liz arrived home from her usual patrol to find Harvey and Edwin sitting on the front porch. She smiled and waved. When she reached the steps, she stopped and leaned a hip against the railing.

"You're up early," Liz said.

"Early to bed, early to rise," Edwin said.

"The early bird gets the worm," Harvey said.

The men laughed at their corny sayings.

"We talked to the others and figured out how to rearrange the patrol shifts. We're doing six, four-hour shifts. There are sixteen of us total, so we're putting two people on each shift. We're rotating days off, so each day, four people have the day off. We blocked it out so that everyone in the same family has the same days off. You can decide how you want to divvy up the actual hours amongst you and the kids," Harvey said.

"We get days off?"

"Yes."

"I wouldn't even know what to do with myself."

"We're thinking of starting a community garden. We're not going to assign shifts unless it really gets going. Most of us had seed packets lying around, so we've planted some winter vegetables. It will be a test run this year, and if the garden produces well enough, we'll do a full-scale planting in the spring," Harvey said.

"Spring…" She shook her head. On one hand, she was glad they were planning ahead, but on the other, she hoped the power outage wouldn't last that long.

"We need to plan ahead. We're already somewhat low on food, but we have enough to get us through the end of the year."

"I don't even know what the date is anymore," she said.

"Carla keeps track. She's got a sixteen-month calendar. She's been marking off the day every night before she goes to sleep."

"I'm glad someone's tracking it. I'd hate to miss the holidays."

"We'll plan a celebration when the time comes," Harvey said. "We actually came over to talk with you about something else. We've been thinking, maybe we should recruit a few more neighbors. There are several houses much deeper into the canyon. I think they're all rental properties, but I figure we should check them out."

"You're not worried about bringing strangers into the group?"

"We wouldn't invite them right away. This would be more of a reconnaissance mission. We really don't know what we'll find out there, but we should take a look. The more information we have about the people around us, the easier it will be to defend our community."

"When did you want to head out?" she asked.

"If you're not busy, we'd like to go now."

"I just got back from the night shift. I was hoping for a nap." In fact, she could hardly wait to fall face-first into the bed. However, she didn't want to rely on their judgment. She could probably trust Edwin, but she didn't know anything about how Harvey made decisions. It would be better if she went with them. "I guess I can sleep later."

"Great."

"Did you bring any weapons?"

"No."

"Do you have any?" she asked.

"I've got my dad's old Colt .45 Peacemaker."

"How much ammo do you have?"

"A few boxes full. I found them in Dad's garage when I was cleaning out the house after he died."

"Sorry to hear about your loss," she said.

"It's been over a decade. He's in a better place now."

"What about you?" She jerked her head toward Edwin.

"No guns. I've only got my two hands."

"Could you shoot one if you had to?"

"Sure. I've done some range shooting. Nothing fancy, but if I aim for center mass, I'd probably land at least one shot."

"Good enough for me. I've got rifles or pistols. Which do you prefer?"

"I'll take a pistol. I've had more practice on those," Edwin said.

"Let me run inside and tell the kids I'm leaving. Give me a second."

Although she probably should have invited them inside, she didn't want them to see all of her guns. Over the years, Luke had amassed a large collection which she'd taken with her when she'd fled their home.

After talking to the kids, she grabbed the Ruger

"I don't hear anything, do you?" she whispered.

"Nothing."

"Let's try knocking. You stand over there and cover me." She pointed to the opposite side of the porch. As Edwin moved into position, she took a breath and let it out.

She knocked once. Twice. Three times.

No footsteps or movement. Maybe it was vacant.

She pointed at the doorknob and motioned like she was going to open it. Edwin's eyes bulged. He shook his head from side to side. She nodded vigorously to indicate she intended to follow through on her plan.

"Wait," he whispered. "Maybe we should go around back first."

"We face the same problem either way. If someone's hiding in there, we're going to be ambushed. I'd rather stay in Harvey's line of sight."

"Okay. Shit. Shit."

"On three. One. Two. Three."

She turned the door and pushed it open. She wasn't prepared for what she found inside.

Liz's eyes went wide as Derek stepped out of the kitchen. The thirty year old ex-Marine pointed a pistol at her.

"Derek?"

"Liz?" He lowered the gun.

"What are you doing here?"

"I could ask you the same since I know this isn't your house." Derek holstered his sidearm.

"You two know each other?" Edwin asked.

"He helped my daughter get to the cabin. She was at UC Irvine when the bombs dropped. As she was walking home, she ran into some terrible men. Derek rescued her and escorted her the rest of the way home." She turned to Derek. "I thought your parents lived several canyons over."

"They do. When I got to their place, I found them roasting marshmallows in the fire pit." He chuckled. "Good ole mom, always trying to make lemonade from lemons. I'm glad to see your husband made it home."

"Oh, no. This is Edwin, one of my neighbors."

"It's nice to meet you," Derek said.

"Likewise."

"Are you doing okay?" she asked Derek.

"Mostly, but my dad's had a terrible headache for the last few days. I've been searching for Aspirin. I don't suppose you have any on you?"

"No, but I have some back at the house. I can spare some. We were planning on searching the rest of the houses, but we can do that later." She glanced at Edwin who gave a slight nod.

"Thank you," Derek said. "My father's not one to

complain, so I'm worried about him. His blood pressure hasn't been great the last few years."

"Is he on any medication for it?" Liz asked.

"He's been on a low dose aspirin for the last year. The doctor wanted to put him on something stronger, but dad hates taking medication."

"I don't think I have low dose."

"Anything will do at this point. He's getting migraines more often than not. He only had a week's worth of aspirin left when the bombs dropped. They didn't make it into town before all the stores were ransacked. We ran out five days ago."

"When did the headaches start?"

"Two days later."

"Hopefully what I have will help." Liz headed toward the front door. "Let me go out first. We have someone outside ready to shoot at the first sign of trouble."

"Go right ahead," Derek said.

After walking out onto the front porch, Liz waved both arms overhead until Harvey came out from behind an oak.

"We've got someone with us," she said. "Don't shoot."

Harvey lowered the rifle as they approached. After a brief introduction, the group walked through the woods back to Liz's house.

"How's Sierra doing?" Derek asked.

"I'd like to strangle her with my bare hands some days." After telling him about the trouble they'd been having with the preacher, she added, "If I catch her sneaking around again, I'll probably lock her in the house until Luke gets back."

"Have you heard from him?" Derek asked.

"Yes. He called a few days ago. He should be home within the next five days or so." *As long as he stays alive*, she silently added.

"He'll make it."

"Thanks for saying that."

"Watch your step," Liz said as they cut a path through the woods toward her house. "I've got caltrops and tripwires spread out."

"Remind me never to try to come over at night," Derek said.

"Why would you come here at night?"

Liz stopped walking and turned to face him. Sure, he'd saved Sierra, but she still didn't know him. She was only giving him some aspirin as a gesture of thanks for helping her daughter.

"I don't plan on it." Derek frowned. "You've got nothing to worry about. If I wanted to steal from you or attack your home, I would have done it already."

"We caught you searching another house," Harvey said.

"Only because I knew it was vacant," Derek said. "I've been staking it out the last twenty-four hours. I wasn't about to break into an occupied house. I'm not a thief."

"Did you happen to check any of the other houses further up the canyon?" Harvey asked.

"Yeah. I almost lost a toe outside one. Whoever's hiding out inside has a hell of an aim. I tried to talk to them, but they were only interested in shooting."

"We were planning on checking the other houses to see if we can round up more people for our group," Liz said. "We figure we'll be stronger once we have better numbers."

"Definitely skip the fourth house up on the right. The green one with white trim."

"What about the others?" Liz asked.

"There are three other houses. Two were vacant."

"What about the third?"

"I couldn't tell. I spread dirt all over the front and back porch then went back a few days later to see if there were any footsteps. It looked as if someone may have walked up the back steps, but I couldn't tell for sure. I need to check that one again."

"Why didn't you break in?" Liz asked.

"Like I said, I'm not a thief. If anyone's living there, I'll leave them alone. I only broke into the vacant ones."

"Did you find anything useful in the other houses?"

"Not really."

She noted his vague answer and decided to ask him again later when they were alone. He didn't know Harvey or Edwin, so he probably didn't trust them enough to share info about what he'd found. She didn't blame him. If she'd found a cache of food or weapons, she wouldn't tell anyone either.

When they reached the cabin, Justice came barreling down the steps. After a sharp woof at the strangers, he looked at Liz.

"Come here, boy."

He scrambled toward her and ran two circles around her legs before flopping onto his back in front of Edwin.

"You want belly rubs?" he asked.

"That's one vicious guard dog you got there," Derek said.

"Justice knows Edwin. Luke used to go camping and fishing with him. They took Justice on some of the camping trips. I'll get the aspirin."

The front door opened and Sierra stepped onto the porch.

"Who are all those—Derek!" She ran down the steps and gave him a hug. "How have you been? How are your parents?"

Liz went inside the cabin while they caught up. She pulled the medical kit from underneath the sink. Several single serving packets of aspirin lined the bottom of the kit. She pulled out ten packets, then added four more. No point in being stingy. They had a huge bottle of aspirin hidden in the shed. They wouldn't run out anytime soon.

When she walked back outside, Harvey and Edwin waved her over.

"We're heading home. I've got watch in a few hours," Edwin said.

"And I need to get back to milk the goats," Harvey said.

"Should we plan on checking the other cabins tomorrow?" she asked.

"Yeah." Harvey's voice dropped to a whisper. "Do you trust this guy?"

"I think so."

"We should check the cabins anyway."

"I agree."

"We can discuss it more at tonight's meeting," Harvey said.

"Sounds good."

As they headed toward Edwin's house, Liz turned to find Sierra and Derek huddled together talking in low tones. She narrowed her gaze. What were they whispering about?

"Sierra was just telling me about how much she likes being grounded." Derek grinned. "You're lucky, Sierra. I probably would have tanned your hide if I was your parent."

"I thought you were on my side." Sierra put her hands on her hips and pouted.

"I don't do sides."

"I can spare these for now." Liz handed him the medication.

"But you have more?"

"Maybe. What did you *really* find up at the other cabins?"

He stared at her for several seconds before a slow smile spread across his face.

"Nothing gets past you, does it?" he asked.

"I'd like to think so." She glanced at Sierra who rolled her eyes and headed back inside the cabin.

"I found some food," he said. "I didn't want to say anything earlier because I don't know those guys."

"How much food?"

"Enough for three people for about a month. Not much, but I've been carrying it back to my parent's home. They didn't have much on hand. I'm worried about our food supply."

"Eventually we're going to have to try to find more. I'm going to plant a garden, but I can't count on it. The weather's been strange."

"Cold."

"Too cold for this time of year."

"Do you think the fallout's blocking out the sun?" he asked.

"Maybe. I don't know. Edwin's got a HAM, but information is spotty at best. No one really knows what's going on."

"We should get ready for winter. If we wait too long, we could be up shit creek without a paddle or a boat."

"It's too bad you live a few canyons over. We could use someone like you in the group," she said.

"Let's stay in touch. Even if we're not neighbors, we might be able to help each other out."

"Sounds good."

After Derek left, Liz sat on the front porch. Gray light filtered through the clouds. Even if she managed to plant a garden, would enough sunlight get through to make it grow? She hated to contemplate another six months without power, but if they didn't start planning for a colder than normal winter, then they could run out of food. She had enough for her family, but what about the others? When their food ran out, could she really turn them away?

She never wanted to be in a position in which she'd have to make that choice. At tonight's meeting she'd broach the subject and see what the others thought. Maybe if they pooled their gardening resources, they could start a community garden. They needed to figure out how to divide up the harvest now before people got desperate. Although she didn't want to set up a bunch of rigid rules, she couldn't see any other way to make the community work. Hopefully everyone else would be on board.

"Yeah. He'll say one thing, then do the opposite of what he said when people aren't watching."

"So you've been spying on him?"

"Yeah." Adam chewed on the edge of his lip. "I keep seeing women who aren't his wife go into his office with him. They close the door. I think..."

"What?"

"I think he's having sex with them."

"Seriously? What a creeper."

"I also found out what's in the shed."

"The one behind the church?"

"They've got guns. A lot of guns."

"How many?" Her heart thudded at the implications.

"I couldn't tell."

"More than ten?"

"At least twenty. Maybe more."

"Why do they need so many guns?" she asked.

"I don't know, but I think we have another problem too."

"What?"

"At the last few meals, we haven't been given as much food. We're eating mostly soup. We used to get several pieces of meat in each bowl, now we're lucky to get one piece. I tried to ask my mom about it, but she said not to worry. I think she's just trying to protect me."

"Have you checked the food supply? Does everyone have their own stockpile, or is it all together?"

"It's all together in the church's kitchen. Mom goes in to bake, but she's not allowed to let anyone else in there to help her. It's weird. I don't understand why other people can't help."

"That is odd. Do you think they're going to run out of food?"

"I don't know. I'm going to follow Turner for a while. He's head of security and Elijah talks to him the most. If anything's going on, he'll know."

"Why don't you just ask him?"

"He's not very friendly."

"What will you do if you run out? Do you have any hidden at your house?" she asked.

"No. After the bombs dropped, Elijah made everyone bring their food to the church. He said we'd be in better shape if we combined everything. Some families had more than others. They're going to be pissed when they find out we're running low."

"Do you have a garden?"

"A small one, but not enough to feed everyone."

She was tempted to tell him about the huge stockpile of food they had in the shed, but what if he told Elijah? She couldn't afford to risk their food supply, no matter how much she liked Adam.

However, they had so much, it couldn't hurt to share a few cans.

"I can bring you a little bit of food," she said.

"You can?"

When his eyes widened, a shimmy of desire wriggled in her belly. He was so much cuter than the guys at school. Of course she'd try to help him out. So far he hadn't mentioned a girlfriend. Maybe he was single, but how could she ask without being obvious?

"If I give you food," she said. "You can't share it with anyone."

"Not even my mom?"

"Of course you can share with her, but not like... your girlfriend."

"I don't have a girlfriend."

"Really?" She learned forward.

"I had one but she broke up with me when she left for college."

"That sucks," she said, while celebrating in her head.

"What about you?"

"Nope."

An awkward silence hung between them for several seconds.

"I should head back," he said. "I don't want Elijah wondering where I went."

"He's pretty controlling."

"He's obsessed with knowing where everyone is at all times. He says it's so that he can keep us safe."

"Be careful. Don't let him catch you sneaking around."

"I will."

"Come back tomorrow and I'll bring food."

Instead of turning to leave, he took a few steps closer.

"I'm glad I ran into you," he said softly. "Sometimes I feel like I don't have anyone I can talk to."

"I feel like that too."

He pulled her into a quick hug then jumped back. He turned and jogged into the forest, leaving her to deal with a rush of longing. She had to find a way to help him. Based on what he'd described, the church was running out of food. How much could she afford to bring him?

After filling the buckets, she walked back to the porch behind the cabin. She carefully dumped water into the opening at the top of the 55 gallon drums. She set down the empty buckets and peeked inside the house. With her mom asleep in bed and her brother on patrol, she could check their food supply. No one would miss a couple of cans. Maybe she could get some beans too.

She opened the shed and stepped inside. Pale slices of light cut through the space between the

"Don't you ever talk to me that way," he growled. "Especially in front of my people."

"You're hurting me."

He released her and wiped his hands on the back of his slacks.

"How much food do we have left?"

"You'd know if you bothered to look every once in a while," she said.

When he backhanded her, the sharp edge of her teeth cut into the back of his knuckles. He pulled his hand back and inspected it. He shook it out.

"Don't make me ask twice."

"We'll be out within a week," she whispered. She held her cheek and averted her gaze. Finally subservient, as any good wife should be.

"Get Turner."

She scurried off, leaving him to pace back and forth behind the shed. He and his chief of security had searched all of the members' homes to make sure they weren't holding anything back. All of the food had been carefully catalogued and stockpiled in the church's kitchen.

Anyone with half a brain would have warned him they were running low, but not Patrice. After fifteen years of marriage, he couldn't remember what had attracted him to her in the first place. He should have divorced her years ago. What a waste of a life. He could have married someone else. Someone sweeter, sexier, and more capable of the tasks assigned to godly women. Someone like Nadine. If only he could put aside his wife and replace her with his mistress. Sure, the congregation might question his choice initially, but in the long run, they'd see he'd made a good decision.

Turner walked up to him.

"Patrice sent me over. She had a handprint on her face." Turner frowned. "What happened?"

"I punished her for putting our community in jeopardy."

"What do you mean?"

"We're running out of food."

"How bad is it?"

"She says we only have a week's worth of food left."

"A week?" Turner's eyes widened. "Why didn't anyone say anything?"

"I don't know, but I plan on talking to Melinda later. She does all the baking. She should have noticed the dwindling supplies."

"What are we going to do about it?"

We, indeed. Elijah's mouth twitched as he suppressed a smile. He could always count on Turner to have his back. As his right-hand man, Elijah could count on Turner to do anything he asked without question. He was a good soldier of righteousness.

"It's time to raid that woman's house," Elijah said.

"The one with the daughter?"

"Yes."

"Well…"

"What?"

"I was hoping we wouldn't have to steal from anyone else. What if we made a trip into town instead?" Turner asked.

"With what vehicle? None of them work. We'd have to go on foot. It would take an entire day."

"But we wouldn't be stealing."

"It's not stealing. We're God's ordained people. We deserve all of the bounty that He has to offer. Have you caught any more squirrels?"

"Not since day before yesterday."

"The forest is barren. There aren't enough big animals to support us. Even if we managed to kill a mountain lion, it would only hold us over for a few days. We need more. We should have been stockpiling food from day one."

"We didn't know how long this would last," Turner said.

"It's the edge of the world. Armageddon, and if we're to make the final stand against darkness, then we need sustenance."

"We can get it from the city. There must be some food left in the city."

"Maybe," Elijah said. "But would it be worth the risk? We could be outgunned. We could run into other groups. Stronger groups. More organized. Larger."

"Our group is as strong as they come," Turner said with conviction.

"Yes, but the army of darkness may be stronger. What would be safer for our people: facing an unknown number of people in town, or facing a handful of people at that woman's house?"

"The house."

"You've been watching it, correct?"

"Yes."

"Have you seen the woman's husband?"

"Not yet," Turner said.

"She's probably divorced. A woman as bull-headed and cocky as she would drive any man away."

"Or he's been inside every time we've been there."

"If he's hiding, then he's a coward. Easily defeated."

"They keep their food in a shed behind the house," Turner said.

"Excellent. If you went at night, could you get in and out without being seen? We don't want a repeat incident of the time your team tried to breach the main house. We lost a good man that day. We can't afford to lose any more."

"We could go tonight. I'll take a couple of the guys with me. From what I can tell, she's got a stockpile of rice and beans, along with some canned food."

"Take as much as you can. Take everything if possible. We'll only have one shot at this. Once she discovers an empty shed, she'll probably realize we were there. I want our perimeter maintained while you're gone. Tell your men to pay special attention to the forest. She's a good shot. With a rifle, she could get us from within the tree line."

"Will do. Anything else?"

"Let's keep this to ourselves. I don't want anyone else to worry about food. It's my job to provide for them, so I'll provide."

After Turner left, Elijah pulled the shed key out from underneath his shirt. He used it to open the door. Inside, a multitude of weapons glinted at the ready. When an army of true believers had God on their side, they were unstoppable. Nothing would go wrong tonight. And tomorrow, they'd celebrate with a feast.

9

Luke held a flashlight in an ice pick-like grip with his left hand, while he pointed the gun with his right hand. Using this technique made it easy to operate the pressure switch at the end the flashlight, and it also gave him the ability to strike downward with the hand holding it.

After scanning each of the rooms on the first floor for threats, he nodded at Boyd. They headed toward the stairs. They'd agreed to remain silent until they could clear the entire building. They could have tried to go floor by floor, hunting for threats as well as food at the same time, but Luke didn't want their attention split between safety and sustenance.

Five floors needed to be cleared. As Luke approached each doorway, he swept the room in a wide arc before entering it to check for hiding places. Everything seemed undisturbed. If he hadn't known that the world was ending, he would have expected to see employees hard at work. Computers, phones, and knickknacks covered desks. Photos of families, pets, and vacation spots hung from cubicle walls.

He'd already spotted multiple food items in plain view, but until they cleared the last closet, they wouldn't relax.

Forty minutes later, Luke was satisfied that they were completely alone.

"Let's start here and work our way back down," Luke said.

"I got dibs on that Three Musketeers bar we passed a minute ago," Boyd said.

"Go for it."

As Boyd trotted off to grab the candy bar, Luke headed toward a desk with a neon-green sports drink. He unscrewed the cap and took a long swig of "Electric Cool," whatever that meant. The chemical aftertaste lingered on his tongue as he searched the drawers for food.

He struck out at the first desk. The second one was a dud too. But the third desk contained a half-eaten beef jerky pack as well as several sticks of gum. He didn't plan on eating the gum, but it would be a nice treat to stave off some of the monotony of walking down the railroad tracks. Although, after everything he'd been through, he could go for a little monotony. He chuckled.

"What's so funny?" Boyd asked as he returned from the other side of the room.

"I was thinking about our situation. A little over a week ago, my biggest worry was a flight delay. Now I'm struggling to find food. I didn't realize how spoiled I'd been. Before the bombs, there was food everywhere. So much food that we were killing ourselves eating too much of it. Now people are out there starving."

"I've got a garden at my house. The wife loves her tomato plants. We've also got a bunch of squash. I swear I've eaten it in every possible form. Baked, grilled, sautéed, stirred into soup. Let me tell you, if you need a plant that goes crazy with a little water, plant some squash."

"I'll keep that in mind," Luke said.

"Does your wife garden?"

"Not really. We've got some flowers, but nothing you can eat."

"Some flowers are edible," Boyd said. "They're not going to keep you from starving, but my wife likes to use them to pretty up dinner."

"What's her name?"

"Vicki."

"Mine's Liz."

"Luke and Liz. Sounds good together."

"How long have you been married?" Luke asked.

"Gosh, must be twenty—no—twenty-two years now. Man, time flies."

"Liz and I have been married twenty years."

"Any kids?" Boyd asked.

"Two. Sierra and Kyle. You?"

"Three. Molly, Dean, and Sam. Molly and Dean are both in college. Sam's got two more years and then he'll be off to college too. Well, if going to college is even an option in two years. How long do you think this thing's going to last?"

"I heard we got hit by an EMP."

"I thought that only happened in movies."

"Apparently not."

"Is it something we can recover from?" Boyd asked.

"Eventually, but it could take years. It depends on how widespread the EMP was. If it only covered part of the continental US, then we could be back online in a year or two if we can get new transformers from overseas."

"And if not?"

"If not…God, I hate to even think about it," Luke said.

"Do you think other countries got hit too?"

"I have no idea. No one knows what's going on. I met a couple of people with HAM radios, but information is spotty and unreliable. Even when we had the internet it was hard to figure out what was real and what was pure speculation or an all-out lie."

"I knew things were getting bad when the politicians started lying about everything," Boyd said.

"All the signs were there."

"I wish I'd stocked up on canned food. I read a bunch of articles about how things could go bad. There were all these shows on TV about how to garden, hunt, and fish, but I never went out and tried any of it. If I can't find enough canned food for my family, we're not going to make it."

Luke listened without comment. Boyd was starting to grow on him, but they weren't friends, and they certainly weren't family, so there was no way he was going to tell Boyd about his stockpile of food. For security reasons, he hadn't even mentioned the city he was headed toward. He'd told Boyd he was heading south, but didn't give any specifics.

"Let's clear this floor then move down one," Luke said. "If you can find a bag or backpack, grab it. Load up as much as you can carry and let's get going. I want to make some more progress before nightfall."

"Okay."

They worked to clean out the fifth floor before

moving down one. On the fourth, Boyd spotted a backpack. After emptying it, he filled it with several pop-top cans of tuna and more energy bars.

The third floor netted a huge water supply. Someone had a pack of twenty-four, eight ounce bottles. They guzzled as much water as they could stand before loading the rest of the bottles into their packs.

On the second floor, they added some peanut butter pretzels to their supply. Boyd munched on a handful as they headed toward the stairs.

"How full is your bag?" Luke asked.

"About half-full," Boyd said between bites.

"I saw a gym across the way. Should we hit that up next?"

"A gym? They don't have any food."

"They might. Usually they have a couple of vending machines or a juice bar with snacks."

"I guess it's worth a shot," Boyd said.

Downstairs, they carefully picked a path through the glass. After checking to make sure the street was clear, they jogged across to the gym. A barbell hung halfway out of the front door. The windows had also been smashed out.

Back on high alert, Luke climbed through the door and swept the room with his flashlight and gun. Unlike the office building, the gym was trashed inside. Shattered shards of mirrors reflected a kaleidoscope of destruction. Weight benches had been tossed across the room. Dumbbells poked holes through the drywall. The only equipment that hadn't been disturbed was bolted to the floor.

"What a mess," Boyd said.

"What a waste. Let's check the locker rooms before we start looking for food."

"Okay."

The locker rooms were silent. No one hid behind any of the doors and the closets were either locked or clear.

"Try to stay away from the front windows," Luke said. "We don't want anyone walking by to spot us."

"Be a ghost. Got it."

Luke smiled. At least Boyd had turned out to be a good travel buddy. So far he'd been pulling his own weight, helping where he could, and standing back while Luke checked for hostiles. At least he'd have someone to talk to for the next thirty miles. They could take turns keeping watch at night and it never hurt to have an extra set of eyes scanning for threats.

For the first time in a long time, Luke relaxed slightly. They hadn't run into any trouble in the last couple of hours. It didn't mean danger wasn't coming, but for now, he felt relatively safe. Hopefully Liz and the kids were relaxing at the cabin. In a few days' time he'd be back at their secluded sanctuary where he'd be able to rest and mentally prepare himself for the long road ahead.

LUKE GRABBED a dumbbell from a weight rack and headed toward the women's locker rooms.

"Where are you going with that?" Boyd asked.

"I need tampons."

"Whoa! Is there something you're not telling me?"

Luke laughed.

"Why tampons?"

"You can use them to plug bullet holes," Luke said.

"I hope you don't plan on getting shot again."

"That's definitely not part of the plan, but I'm out of gauze. Medical supplies are scarce already. I want to get them while I can."

"Well you're in luck. I found a first aid kit in one of the desks."

"Nice score."

"Let's see what we've got in here." Boyd opened the metal box and began poking through the contents. "A few Band-Aids, antibiotic cream, alcohol cleansing pads, aspirin, and a butterfly wound closure."

"I hope we don't need any of it, but I'm glad we have it."

"Me too. What did you find so far?"

"I picked up a cigarette lighter, a pencil, and some garbage bags," Luke said.

"A pencil? What are you going to do with that?"

"When I was a kid I had a buddy who really liked to play with fire. A bit of a pyro if you ask me. One day we were in the garage with an old car battery and jumper cables. He asked if I wanted to see something cool. I was about thirteen at the time so I was ready for anything. So he hands me a pencil and an X-ACTO knife."

"I can't wait to hear where this is headed," Boyd said.

"He tells me to scrape all of the paint off the outside of the pencil. I do. Then he tells me the lead inside is a mixture of graphite and clay. I couldn't give two shits about the pencil, but he liked to explain every detail of his crazy experiments, so I go along with it."

"Smile and nod."

"Yep. Anyway, he tells me the lead will catch on fire if you hit it with an electrical current."

"I see where this is headed," Boyd said.

"So he clips the red cable to one end of the pencil and the black cable to the other. Then he hooks them up to the battery. Red to the positive, black to the negative."

"Or switch them up for a real fireworks display." Boyd grinned.

"Not if you value your life."

"It's not like the thing's going to explode."

"No, but it will spark like crazy."

"Another way to get a fire started."

"Remind me never to put you in charge of starting the fire," Luke grumbled.

"So what happened?"

"So he hooks up the jumper cables to the battery and boom! The whole pencil bursts into flames."

"I want to try that right now," Boyd said.

"If you have a pair of jumper cables and a battery stashed somewhere, we could do it."

"I'm fresh out."

"Same here. But I figured it wouldn't hurt to hang onto the pencil just in case."

"Let's hit up an auto supply place next. I've got to see this pencil exploding thing," Boyd said.

"I want to keep moving south. You can try it once you get home."

"Buzz kill."

"Pyro."

"You said you grabbed trash can liners too?"

"Yeah. You can use them as rain gear, for water collection, ground cover, a sun shade, a blanket—"

"Okay, MacGyver. I get it," Boyd said.

"You've got to start thinking outside the box. We're used to having specialized tools and equipment for every possible scenario. But those days will be over soon. When you can't go to the store to get a lighter, how will you start a fire? When you can't get new roof tiles for your house, how will you keep rain out?"

"You're assuming it'll rain in Southern California."

"The drought's been bad," Luke said. "But one day it will end and we might be flooded. All it takes is one El Niño year. Remember '97 and '98? Thirty-five counties were declared federal disaster areas. Seventeen people died."

"I remember thinking I might need a canoe to get to work."

"That was a bad winter."

"And you think a few trash bags would make a difference if it happened again?" Boyd asked.

"Maybe. Maybe not. But I'd rather have extra trash bags just in case."

"Do you really think things are going to get that bad?" Boyd asked.

"I hope they don't, but if we really did get hit with an EMP, we're going to be without power for at

"Sorry," he whispered.

The back door of the gym burst open and three gangbangers spilled out, AKs in hand.

"Don't move," Luke whispered as he ducked behind the car.

"Enrique, you're trippin', homes. There ain't nobody back here," one banger said.

"I saw them, man. That guy from the warehouse. They were inside a minute ago," Enrique said.

"I don't see nothing," the third guy said. "Let's go."

When they disappeared back into the building, Luke nudged Boyd.

"Those were the same guys who had me trapped in the warehouse yesterday."

"The ones who shot you?"

"Grazed me," Luke said.

"Grazed, shot. Shit's all the same."

"Not even close."

"You've been shot before?"

"Yeah, and I'll tell you all about it after we get the hell out of here."

10

The campfire snapped and hissed as Harvey set another log on the fire. Liz leaned back in the plastic lawn chair and fought against the need to continue to argue her point. So far, no one was interested in pooling resources. She'd tried approaching the issue from every possible angle, to no avail. Half of the group didn't believe the blackout would last longer than a month or two. The other half didn't want to redistribute their wealth. She couldn't blame them; who wanted to face the reality of months, maybe years without power? Still, if they waited too long to come up with a plan, it could be too late.

"Does anyone else have anything they want to say before we end the meeting?" Harvey asked.

"I want to address Liz's point about pooling

resources," Edwin said. "I do think she has a point. Now I know we can't come to an agreement right now, but I'd like you to consider what she said. We're stronger together than if we keep everything separate."

"Why should we have to share our food?" Irene asked. "I worked hard for months canning everything from my garden."

"But do you have enough soap?" Edwin asked.

"What does soap have to do with anything? You can't eat soap."

"No, but what if you run out of soap and Liz has some?"

"Then we can trade," Irene said.

"That would require negotiation, and the more we have to negotiate with each other, the more issues we're going to stir up. Wouldn't it be better if we had a common pool of resources to choose from?" Edwin asked.

"What would keep Liz from taking all of my tomatoes?" Irene flashed her a perturbed look. "She could get up one day and decide she needs every last jar of strawberry jam."

"I don't like strawberries." Liz couldn't keep the sarcasm from her voice. Irene never listened to reason. She seemed determined to fight Liz at every turn. Liz couldn't understand the other woman's hostility.

"Fine, then my blueberry jam. You know what I meant," Irene said.

"Why don't we table this discussion for tomorrow? We'll give everyone a chance to really consider the long-term impact this decision might have on the group," Edwin said.

"Sounds good to me," Franklin said. "Is the meeting over? I want to get home."

"We're adjourned," Harvey said.

Liz stood and waited as the other neighbors filtered out of the circle.

"Sorry about my wife," Harvey said softly. "I don't know what's gotten into her. Your solution sounds perfectly reasonable."

"We need to think about the future. If this thing ends up lasting through the winter, we'll be forced to share food whether we like it or not."

"I know. Let me talk to her. I'll see if I can get her to change her mind."

"Good luck reasoning with her."

"See you tomorrow." Harvey chuckled and gave Liz a playful pat on the shoulder as he walked past.

Liz took the long way back to her cabin. After spending the last hour arguing what should have been an obvious solution, she needed to cool off. Fortunately the plummeting temperature helped.

Eventually the others would understand the need

long. If she didn't chase the thieves immediately, she'd never get the cans back. Pooling resources with the neighbors would be a moot point. If she didn't have anything to offer, why would they entertain her idea for a second longer than it took to reject it?

She stepped out from behind the tree and glanced at the cabin. The windows remained covered, the lights out. As long as they stayed barricaded in the cabin, they'd be safe.

She trekked through the woods, searching for the thieves. Although she had a damn good idea of where they were headed, she needed to be sure they hadn't taken a side route.

After combing through the woods for several minutes, she crossed the stream. Fresh boot prints disturbed the mud. Of course. The preacher's men. They were headed directly toward the compound. Without backup, she couldn't confront them without catastrophic risk. Nevertheless, she followed their trail until it terminated at the compound.

Two men dragged a third man between them. One of the men also pulled a wagon full of food across the road toward the church's picnic area.

Damn them.

Outnumbered and outgunned, she couldn't charge down to reclaim her property. She'd have to wait for reinforcements. Hopefully once she told the group about the robbery, they'd offer to help get the food back. She couldn't do it alone. It would be a suicide mission.

As she backed into the shadows, her spine went rigid. If the preacher wanted war, he'd get it.

ELIJAH TAPPED his fingers against the picnic table where he sat waiting for his men to return. They'd been gone for over three hours, much longer than they should have needed. He'd considered going into the forest to see where they were, but didn't want to risk being shot by friendly fire.

A quarter moon hung over the sky, throwing off enough light to outline figures approaching the edge of the forest.

Elijah's jaw dropped. Not again.

Turner half-carried a man onto the road. Ivan trailed behind with a wagon full of food. He held a pistol in his free hand while his head swiveled from side to side.

"Help me," Turner said.

Elijah ran over and hooked Rory's arm over his shoulder. Rory, one of the younger men in the group, had insisted on helping on this mission. Initially, Elijah had been against it. He only wanted seasoned men on the team, but Turner had insisted on giving the young man a chance.

"What happened?" Elijah asked.

"He's been shot. We need to get him into the house."

"Take him to mine."

As they approached his house, several yards behind the church, Melinda stepped out of the shadows.

"What's going on? Is that blood?" she asked.

"Either help, or get out of the way," Elijah snapped.

Melinda scurried to the front door and opened it. She held it as Elijah and Turner pulled Rory into the room.

"Shut the door," Elijah said.

"What happened?" she asked.

"He was shot," Turner said.

"How?"

"Get him on the kitchen table," Elijah said.

"What's all the commo—" Patrice stopped just outside the threshold to the bedroom. "Is that Rory?"

"Go get Kat," Elijah commanded.

As Patrice ran to get the nurse, Melinda grabbed a pair of scissors from the counter. She quickly cut away his shirt to reveal a gaping wound in the upper left quadrant of his chest.

Adrenaline spiked through Elijah's stomach. He pressed his hands against the flow of blood.

"Get a towel."

Melinda grabbed a towel and handed it to him.

The door opened and Kat rushed into the room.

"Again?" she said.

Melinda's gaze snapped to Kat. "What do you mean *again*?"

Elijah shot Kat and Turner a death-glare. If they opened their mouths, he'd be forced to get rid of everyone in the room. He couldn't allow the congregation to find out two members had died while they were attempting to infiltrate that woman's property.

Patrice stood in silent condemnation, judgment smeared across her face. When he glared, she scurried into the bedroom like a field mouse.

"Get a bowl of hot, clean water," Kat said, breaking the uncomfortable silence.

As Melinda headed into the kitchen, Elijah glanced at Turner, who mumbled a prayer under his breath.

"He's not going to make it," Elijah said. "He's lost too much blood."

"I need more light," Kat said.

"I found a flashlight on the counter," Melinda said. "Here's the water."

She set a bowl of steaming water on the table.

"Exactly," Elijah said. "They're casualties in a holy war."

"He's not dead yet. Have some faith," Turner said.

"Of course," Elijah said.

"Shit!" Kat dropped the tweezers. They clattered against the table. An ever-increasing pool of blood dripped over the edge onto the wood floor. "I'm losing him. He's lost too much blood."

Elijah stood back so he wouldn't get blood on his loafers. He plastered a concerned expression on his face to mask pure rage. *She* had done this. Liz. She'd cast a dark shadow over his congregation. She'd brought death and discord into his life and if she didn't stop, he'd have to find a way to get rid of her for good.

"He's gone," Kat said. She stepped back, tears in her eyes. "He was just a kid."

"He was twenty-two if I'm not mistaken," Elijah said.

"A kid." She shook her head and turned toward the door.

"Kat."

"What?"

"Remember what I said about keeping it quiet?"

"I won't tell a soul."

"Thank you. I'm glad I can count on you."

She nodded briefly before leaving him alone with

Turner. A second later, Melinda rushed back into the room. She carried a medicine bottle.

"I found—" She stopped when she spotted Rory on the table. "Did he…"

"Kat did everything she could. It was too late. Where did you get that?" he asked, nodding at the bottle.

"In the church, by the medical kit."

"I'll put it back."

He held out his hand. When she didn't immediately hand it over, he arched a brow.

"I saw Ivan take a wagon full of food into the kitchen. Where did it come from?" she asked.

"That's none of your concern."

"Did it come from Liz's house?"

"Yes."

"I'm guessing she didn't give it to you."

"She's an instrument of the devil trying to break our group apart. We deserve the food more than her. We're doing God's work."

"Are we?" she asked.

"Of course. Besides, where else do you expect us to find food? Do you want to starve?"

"Why don't you go into town?"

"The stores have been looted. There's nothing left."

"How do you know that? You haven't left this place since the bombs dropped."

"My scouts have checked," he lied. Sending his team out on a dangerous mission just to confirm what he already knew was pointless. "There's nothing left."

"What will we do when that food runs out? There wasn't enough for more than a month or two. We've got over forty mouths to feed."

"God always provides."

"I think you stole it. That's why Rory got killed. You were trespassing."

"Maybe you'll feel differently about this after you've felt the true pain of hunger. If I hear you spread rumors about what happened tonight, if you complain to anyone, you'll miss tomorrow night's food. Adam will too."

"You can't do that to my son."

"The sins of the mother pass down to the son."

"Since when?"

Blood rushed in to scald his cheeks. He clenched his fists by his sides.

"No food tomorrow."

"But—"

"Keep talking, and you won't eat for two days. I suggest you shut your mouth and leave. If you tell anyone about tonight, there will be consequences."

She glared at him defiantly for a second before her

shoulders dropped. As she left, she slammed the door behind her.

He smirked. She needed him far more than he needed her. Eventually he'd weed the weak sheep from his flock. For now, he needed numbers to maintain the family-like atmosphere. But with war coming, he needed to build an army. Turner would know where to find capable men. And he'd know where to hide a body.

breath caught under her ribcage, as if a fully inflated balloon had been jammed up against it. She forced herself to take deeper breaths. Lack of oxygen wouldn't do any good.

She stepped off the porch and slowly circled around toward the shed. The door hung open. Inside, a mess of tangled gardening equipment and broken jars of food littered the floor. She bent down to retrieve a can of peaches from under the workbench. A second can filled with green beans lay on its side, dented, but otherwise intact.

As she opened the storage area, her heart sank. Bare shelves. They'd taken everything, even the rice and beans.

Unable to accept the level of devastation, she continued to search through the shed, hoping against hope they'd moved the beans and rice. They couldn't have taken everything in one trip. They had to have made multiple trips. Either way, they'd taken everything except for the two discarded cans.

She leaned against the wall. Tears brimmed in her eyes. The bags of rice and beans inside the house wouldn't last longer than a few days. A week tops. She'd been prepared, but it hadn't mattered. In less than an hour, she'd lost everything. How was she going to tell the kids?

As she wiped at the dampness on her cheeks, the

weight of being in charge of her family crushed down like a thousand-pound boulder. She needed Luke. If he'd been home, none of this would have happened. She should have brought all of the food inside. She should have forced the group to keep guards on patrol at all times.

Determined not to fall into a pit of despair, she pushed off the wall. Eventually they would have run out of food anyway and they would have needed to come up with a solution. This has simply moved up the timeline. Instead of waiting months to figure out how to get more food, the group would have to figure it out now.

She locked the shed and headed back into the cabin. Once inside, she went into the kitchen and set the cans of peaches and green beans on the counter. The kids watched in silence as she pulled a can of ravioli out of the cupboard.

"How bad is it?" Sierra asked softly.

"We're having ravioli for dinner."

"You didn't answer the question."

Liz sighed as she dumped the gelatinous goo into a pot. She carried it out onto the back porch and fired up the barbeque. The kids joined her.

"We're low on food," Liz said. "I'm going to talk to the others and see what we can do about it. I know there's more food in the community."

"Do you think they'll give it to us?" Kyle asked.

"Yes," she said with more conviction than she felt.

After the squabble they'd had about sharing food earlier that night, she wasn't convinced anyone would be willing to give up their stash. She'd have to find a way to convince them that it would somehow benefit the whole community.

She finished heating the ravioli and dished it into three bowls. Normally she fed them twice as much food, but until she could rebuild their supply, she'd have to ration what they had.

As she handed Sierra a bowl, her daughter eyed it and cast a questioning look at Liz as if to say, *where's the rest of it?*

Kyle mumbled a "Thank you" before heading inside with his bowl. They ate at the dining table in somber silence. Although she hadn't spelled out the dire nature of the situation, they had to know. They were smart enough to see how much food they had in the cabinets.

Instead of shoveling food into her mouth, Liz savored each bite of ravioli. The tinny, processed quality of the food didn't bother her the way it normally would have. For now, she was grateful to have anything to eat.

Before the bombs dropped, she hadn't given her ability to get food at will a second thought. The grocery store by her house never closed. If she wanted pizza and beer at two a.m., she could have it. Craving a bag of tortilla chips? Done. Jonesing for a full-sugar Coke? Why not?

Now none of that was possible. And even worse, it could be years before grocery stores were fully operational again. *Years.*

Was anything left out there, or had it all been ransacked already? Should she have gone into town sooner to try to get whatever she could for her family? If she went to the store now, what would she find?

"I'm going to Edwin's," she said. "I need to talk to him about our next move."

"Are you going to take everything back from the preacher?" Sierra asked.

"They have too many men and too many guns," Liz said. "We don't have enough people to run a raid."

"How are you going to find more food?" Kyle asked.

"The others might have some at their houses. Or, we might have to take a trip into town."

"Is that safe?" Sierra asked.

"I don't know. If we did go into town, I'd bring other men from the group. We'd be able to carry more out if we did it together."

"Do you think they'll agree?" Kyle asked.

"I hope so."

"So the men will go with me while the women keep guard?"

"Sounds fair," Burt's wife Tawney said. "Are you going on foot, or do you want to try to take the truck?"

"You have a running truck?" Liz's eyebrows shot up.

Burt flashed a frustrated look at his wife before responding. "We've got an old Chevy in the garage. We tried starting it up the other day and it worked."

"Why didn't we hear it?" Harvey asked.

"The garage is soundproof. The wife didn't want to hear me banging around in there, so I soundproofed it two years ago," Burt said.

"How much gas do you have?" Liz asked. "I'd hate to get to town then not have enough to get back."

"I've got a full tank and a five-gallon container's worth."

"That should be plenty."

"Should we leave now?" Harvey asked.

"I think it might be safer than trying to go during the day," she said. "We'll drive with the lights out as much as possible. If we cut through Portola Hills, we can check Foothill Ranch first."

"Walmart. Target. Ralphs. Lots of options," Harvey said. "I like it."

"We can be there and back in a couple of hours, depending on what we find," she said.

"Provided we don't run into any trouble," Franklin said.

"Right." She ignored the flutter of nerves in her belly. "We should bring guns. At least two each. Extra ammo too. Just in case."

The three men nodded.

"We'll meet at Burt's place in, let's say, an hour?"

"Sounds good," Harvey said.

AN HOUR LATER, they piled into the truck. Liz rode shotgun, literally, while Harvey and Franklin sat in the truck bed. Burt drove. They kept the lights off and drove slowly. After turning onto Santiago Canyon Road, they headed for Portola Hills. The occasional pop of a gun splintered the night. When they reached the community's clubhouse area, the hair on the back of her neck stood on end.

A bonfire blazed in the clubhouse parking lot. Flickering light illuminated groups of men who sat around the fire. Several held beer bottles. Others sat with shotguns resting on their thighs. Not good.

"Speed up," Liz whispered.

They couldn't go around the clubhouse without

having to backtrack for several miles. They couldn't afford to waste any gas, so they had to keep going.

"No matter what happens, don't stop," she said.

"Got it."

Burt accelerated toward the parking lot. They were only a hundred yards away when several men set their beers down. At fifty yards, men hoisted their shotguns and headed toward the road.

"Punch it," Liz said.

The truck lurched forward. She grabbed the bar over the window with one hand to steady herself.

As they raced past the bonfire, several men called out, yelling at them to stop. When they opened fire, Harvey and Franklin shot back. Men ran every which way, slamming into each other before recovering and aiming for the truck.

Several men ran after them. Burt whipped the truck around a bend in the road, fishtailing before regaining control. The steep, downhill grade helped their momentum. Shots pinged off the roof of the cab.

The truck flew down the hill. Burt slammed on the brakes, trying to get control as they weaved around a pile of smoldering debris. As they approached the end of the road, Liz grabbed the door handle. She prayed he could slow the truck enough to keep it from flipping.

Screeching tires and groaning metal accompanied their partially airborne flight around the intersection. When all four wheels made contact, air blasted from her lungs. She sucked in a breath as the truck skidded to a stop on an empty road.

"Jesus that was close." He lifted his shaky hands off the wheel and scrubbed his face. "You guys okay back there?"

"Fine."

"Good."

"You're not hit?" Liz asked.

"No. Damn near close," Harvey said. "But we're good to keep going. I don't think we should sit here too long. We're only a mile or so away. They could try to follow us."

"Do you think it's safe enough to go to the shopping center?" Burt asked.

"I don't know," Liz said. "But we have to check it out."

"Okay. But if it looks like trouble, we're leaving."

"Okay." She didn't like it, but she couldn't force the others to risk their lives for her. "Let's start at Walmart."

Burt nodded and put the truck back into gear. An empty road took them through a small industrial area. They passed one section of the shopping center.

12

Luke peeked into the rear window of a nondescript house. The window whipped open and he stared down the barrel of a shotgun.

"You boys best move on now," the homeowner said. "The wife hates cleaning guts off this damn window."

"Shit."

Luke grabbed Boyd's sleeve and took off running. After crossing the yard, he used a crate propped up against the back fence to vault over. Boyd followed on his heels.

"That went well," Boyd said as they ran across a backyard.

"I thought so."

"Now what?"

"We need a new plan."

"Ya think?"

Luke raced up to a wooden gate. Fortunately it wasn't locked. He unlatched it and pulled it open. After Boyd cleared the gate, Luke closed it. They hurried across the front lawn and onto the sidewalk. Luke slowed his pace so that they wouldn't draw undue attention.

"Where should we go?" Boyd asked.

"We need to get away from the populated areas."

"We're in the middle of Riverside. There are probably a hundred thousand people within a stone's throw of us. I'm starting to think we're screwed."

"That's ridiculous. No matter how bad things get, there's always a way out. I have an idea, but it's going to sound crazy," Luke said.

"What?"

"We should go underground."

"What?" Boyd's eyebrows shot up.

"Last night I slept in a library. I found a map of the storm drain system for Riverside County."

"Storm drains? You've got to be kidding me. They're full of nasty-ass water and rats and shit."

"You're thinking of the sewer system, it's not the same."

"Are you sure?" Boyd asked.

"Pretty sure."

"I'm not crawling down into a hole unless absolutely necessary. I'll take my chances above ground. It's not like those guys shot at us. We got away."

"The guy at the house almost shot me," Luke said. "I got lucky. If someone was trying to break into my house, I'd shoot him."

"That's cold."

"It's realistic. Before shit hit the fan, I wouldn't have considered it. It would have been considered illegal in California."

"Even if the guy's breaking in?" Boyd asked.

"Yep. The law says you have to be in imminent danger of death or great bodily injury in order to justify deadly force."

"I'd consider someone breaking into my house as a threat to my life."

"I agree, but that *was* the law," Luke said.

"Was?"

"There's no law anymore. The laws of the past are over. Do you see any cops around?"

"I haven't seen one since Vegas."

"Exactly."

"Without laws, what's to keep anyone from simply taking whatever they want?" Boyd asked.

"Nothing. Without anyone to enforce the law, criminals will be even more dangerous now."

"Is that why you want to go in the storm drains?"

"I figure it's the safest route at this point," Luke said.

"Shouldn't we take advantage of daylight to get as far away from here as possible?" Boyd asked.

"I think we should go underground for now. It might slow us down, but it should be relatively safe."

"When we run into a writhing mass of rabid rats, I'll remind you that you said that."

"Trust me, rats are the least of our worries. If we run into those gangbangers again, we'll probably end up needing those tampons."

"What…oh, right. Bullet plugs." Boyd grinned. "I haven't needed a tampon before and I sure as hell hope I'll never need one."

"Same here."

"What about your leg?" Boyd pointed at the bandage on Luke's leg. "Aren't you worried about bacteria? Those drainage systems are petri dishes."

"I've got it wrapped up pretty good. I can put a trash bag around it for extra protection."

"It's still asking for trouble. You can't walk into a hospital if it gets infected."

"I know, but we might be able to find antibiotics later," Luke said.

"Don't count on it."

"I'll be fine."

"Stay here and man the flashlight while I put it back," Luke said. He quickly ascended the ladder. He struggled against the weight of the manhole cover. From this angle, he'd expected to be able to slide it back into place. No such luck.

"Told you it wouldn't be easy," Boyd said.

"Just keep the damn flashlight pointed up here."

As Luke yanked on the paracord, the steel cover moved another inch. Trying to get leverage inside such a small hole wasn't easy. He'd resorted to pulling an inch at a time.

"That's close enough," Boyd said.

"No. All the way or someone will know we're down here."

After he'd finally pulled the damn cover into place, Luke wiped his forehead with the back of his hand. Musty air stagnated in the tunnel. Curved cement walls stretched into darkness in both directions. Odd echoes reverberated from farther in the tunnels. A trickle of running water dripped from a distant source.

"This is creepy as hell," Boyd said.

Luke didn't respond, but silently agreed. Maybe this wasn't the best idea, but it beat running around topside.

"Let's get this over with," Luke said.

As they headed into the tunnel, the yellow glow

of the flashlight illuminated discolored brick walls. The gray remnants of an old waterline marked a place three quarters of the way up the walls. Unless there was a flash flood, they would be okay. *Please don't let it rain*, Luke prayed.

After two uneventful miles, Luke relaxed his guard. The tension in his shoulders eased and he continued at a less cautious pace. As they rounded a corner, the absolute darkness beyond the reach of his light shifted. He quickly killed the light.

"What—"

"Shh!" Luke hissed.

"What is it?" Boyd whispered.

In the distance, a light bobbed up and down. With each passing second, it moved closer. If they attempted to run, they wouldn't make it far. There wasn't anywhere to hide. The last section of the tunnel had been so straight that any idiot who could squeeze a trigger would be able to send a kill shot right into their backs.

Luke switched the flashlight to his left hand. He retrieved his gun and aimed. Blinded by the oncoming light, he held a hand up to cover his eyes. Voices echoed against the walls of the storm drain.

"Whoa! There's more people down here," someone said. He sounded young, possibly Kyle's age.

"Dude, that guy's got a gun."

"Hey, don't shoot!" the first kid yelled.

"Turn your flashlight off," Luke said.

"O...Okay."

The light went out, plunging the tunnel into darkness. Luke flicked on his light. Two boys in their early teens lifted their hands over their heads. They were dressed in filthy jeans and ripped T-shirts. Neither looked as if they'd had a bath in weeks.

"Please don't shoot us," the first teen said.

"Keep your hands up or I will shoot you," Luke warned. "Boyd, check them for weapons."

As Boyd searched the teens, Luke kept his finger off the trigger, but ready. If things went south, he wanted to get the first shot on target. Age didn't mean a damn thing anymore. A thirteen-year-old could pull a trigger just as fast as any adult, maybe faster.

"They're clean," Boyd said.

"What are you doing down here?" Luke asked.

"Just having fun," the second teen said. "I'm Mason, this is Noah."

"Are you brothers?" Boyd asked.

"No. Friends. How about you guys?" Mason asked.

"Friends." Boyd cast a quick glance at Luke.

"Can we put our hands down yet?" Noah asked.

"Sure," Luke said.

"What are you guys doing down here?" Mason asked.

"We're on our way home," Luke said.

"Why aren't you walking on the street?" Noah asked.

"It's not safe," Boyd said.

"It's not," Noah said softly, a shadow passing across his face. Luke had seen that haunted look before on the battlefield. This kid had seen something go terribly wrong.

"What happened?" Luke asked.

Noah shot him a wary gaze before dropping his chin to his chest. He shook his head slowly. Mason took a protective step in his direction.

"His parents got killed," Mason said.

Luke inhaled a breath and blew it out slowly while he waited for the kid to continue.

"It happened four days ago."

"Five," Noah corrected.

"Five. He was home with his parents. It was before all the lights went out. They were watching a movie since none of the TV channels were working."

Luke glanced at Boyd, who stood ramrod straight.

"The movie was almost over when they heard a noise outside. His dad went to check it out and got shot in the head. The guys rushed in and killed his mom. They were going to kill him too, but he ran."

"I should have stayed. I should have tried to help them," Noah said, pain strangling his voice.

"I already told you there was nothing you could do about it," Mason said. "Nobody lives after taking a head shot. They died instantly."

"You don't know that for sure," Noah said.

"Yeah, I do."

"How do you know?" Noah asked in an angry tone.

"In *Call of Duty*, everyone dies when you shoot them in the head. Everybody knows that."

"I should have gone back."

Boyd stepped forward and put his hand on the kid's shoulder. "You did what you had to do to stay alive. Mason's probably right. Those guys probably would have killed you too if you'd stayed."

"Fine. Whatever," Noah grumbled.

"Where are you staying now?" Luke asked.

"With Mason and his mom."

"No dad?" Boyd asked.

"Nope. He took off when I was five and never came back. My mom hates his guts," Mason said.

"She really does," Noah said. "But she's cool. She doesn't care where we go as long as we get home before dark. She gets pissed if we're out after sunset."

"You should listen to her," Luke said. "What are you two doing in the tunnels? You could get trapped down here. If it rains, it's going to flood the pipes. You'll drown."

"It's cool down here. We won't get lost or anything because we always bring chalk with us to mark the path. See?" Mason pulled a large hunk of orange chalk out of his back pocket.

"Even if you mark the path, it's not safe," Boyd said.

"At least no one's shooting at us down here," Noah said.

"True that," Mason said.

"Well... just be careful. Your mom's counting on you to get home safely," Luke said.

"We'll be careful," the boys said in unison.

"Jinx!"

"I said it first!"

"No you didn't!"

"Hey! Knock it off," Luke said in the tone he reserved for disciplining his kids. After several seconds of heavy silence, he cleared his throat. As much as he wanted to help the kids in some way, they weren't his responsibility.

"We've been walking for a while. What are the cross streets here?" Luke asked.

"Uh, I think Magnolia and Jackson," Mason said.

"By the hospital?" Boyd asked.

"Yeah. There's a ton of cops up there," Mason said.

"Why?" Luke asked.

"One of the gangs took over the hospital. It was crazy. There are old people wandering around in the streets—"

"Dead people too," Noah interjected. "Not like wandering around. Not zombies. They're still alive. But yeah, they're all over."

"All over where?" Boyd asked.

"The dead people are piled up on the lawn and shit," Mason said. "It smells like ass."

"Worse than ass," Noah said while wrinkling his nose.

"Where did the bodies come from?" Luke asked.

"From everywhere. People are bringing dead bodies to the hospital when they die. The cops aren't helping. They're trying to get control of the hospital again," Mason said.

"Yeah, they're shooting the place up. I heard someone say they're going to blow it up because there's a bunch of oxygen in there," Noah said.

"Is the backup generator still on?" Luke asked.

"The what?" Noah asked.

"Are the lights still on?"

"Yeah. At night. They're the only ones with lights anymore. The power's out all over the place."

"What time is it right now?"

"Uh, maybe five p.m."

"By now it's probably six," Mason said. "We need to head back home."

"You guys take care of each other and take care of your mom. The world's only going to get more dangerous as people run out of food."

"We've still got a ton of macaroni and cheese," Mason said.

"We stole it from Costco."

"Shh!" Mason slapped Noah's arm.

"They're not going to bust us. They're not cops."

"Be careful out there," Luke said. "Stockpile as much food as you can and don't tell anyone else about what you have. If people find out about your mountain of macaroni and cheese, they'll come and take it from you."

"That would suck," Mason said.

"Exactly. So be safe. Find as much food as you can, and pray."

"Mom says she's been praying to the Great Spaghetti Monster in the sky."

"The what?" Boyd asked.

"She said it's like God but not God. I don't get it," Noah said.

"Keep praying," Luke said. "But don't wait

around for God to save you. He's probably got another million people in line ahead of you."

"We can take care of ourselves," Mason said. "Come on, let's go. See ya around."

As the kids took off down the tunnel, Mason switched on his flashlight to illuminate the streak of orange chalk on the wall. At least they seemed to be somewhat resourceful. Hopefully they'd find a way to survive.

13

Elijah puffed up his chest as yet another member of his flock knocked on the door to his office. He'd lost count of the number of people who'd come by to thank him for the feast. Losing a member of the family seemed less important this morning. He now had the complete respect of his flock, which is what he'd always wanted.

He waved in the elderly married couple who waited patiently at the door. As he half-listened to their praises, he ran through a roster of everyone in the church. Since the bombing, he'd lost two strong, younger men to that woman. He needed more people, but how could he find more? It's not like he could put an ad online. He'd have to talk to Turner about it.

"Excellent. Now, I don't want any thugs or drug addicts."

"I doubt there are any drugs left out there."

"You never know."

"What should I be looking for?"

"Soldiers. Ex-military. Muscle. I'd start over at Cook's Corner."

"Why there?"

"It used to be a big meeting place for men. Maybe they're still meeting there."

"How many should I bring back?"

"Food is scarce for now. Let's start with five. After we're able to go on supply runs, we can add more."

"Seems simple enough."

"On the surface, but I don't want just anyone," Elijah said. "In order to join our community, they need to be able to bring enough food to feed forty people for a week. No less."

"How could they possibly transport that much alone?"

"That's part of the challenge. If you can find a group of five that will work together, even better. They would need to bring five weeks' worth of food. It would be ideal if we could find five men who already know each other, but I don't know what it's like out there."

"What if I can't find five?"

"Can't?" Elijah sat back and steepled his fingers in front of his chest. "I have complete faith in you. I expect that you won't return with less than five capable soldiers. We're depending on you. *I'm* depending on you."

"Sir, I won't let you down."

"Good." Elijah stood and gestured toward the door. "Please close it behind you. I'll be praying for you. Godspeed."

After Turner left, Elijah returned to his desk. He took a key out of his pocket and used it to open the bottom drawer. He retrieved a bottle of twenty-year-old scotch. He poured two fingers' worth into a glass and kicked it back.

As he refilled the glass, a knock sounded on the door. He quickly placed the glass in the top drawer and hid the bottle.

"Come in."

When Melinda walked into the room, he suppressed a groan. She'd been a thorn in his side ever since her son had started cavorting with that girl, Sierra. If he could find a reason to get rid of them, he would, but the family was too small and he couldn't afford to lose any more members. Not yet anyway.

"How can I help you?"

"You can starve me all you want, but you can't starve my son."

"I didn't starve him, you did. I warned you not to disobey me, but you did anyway. For that, you had to be punished."

"Sooner or later people are going to see what you're doing."

"Really?" He leaned forward. "Please, enlighten me. What am I doing?"

"You're trying to turn this place into a cult."

"A cult? Never," he snapped. "I know what a cult looks like and this isn't it."

"That's exactly what this is."

"You're free to go anytime you want to leave. If this was a cult, I'd force you to stay. Have I forced you to do anything?"

"You starved us."

"Humph. Let's just agree to disagree. Anything else? I'm very busy right now."

"Adam and I are going to eat dinner tonight."

"Of course you are. Your penance will be over. I hope you learned your lesson."

"What's wrong with you?" she asked so softly he almost didn't hear her.

"Excuse me?"

"Nothing."

"Good. I'll see you at dinner."

He walked around the desk to the door and held

it open. As soon as she crossed the threshold, he slammed it shut.

Bitch! How dare she talk to him like that? She was the kind of person he wanted to weed out as soon as possible. He didn't need her, or her lazy son.

He headed back to the desk and pulled out the glass as well as a notepad. As he sipped his drink, he drew a line down the center of the page. He made a list of everyone in the church. He listed the expendables on the left side, the assets on the right.

Although he wasn't sure how he was going to thin the herd, he would have to do it at some point. He only wanted the strongest people. The best people. The chosen ones. And if he had to break a commandant to get his way, then so be it. God would forgive him.

ELIJAH STOOD next to the smoldering barbecue while everyone else threw away their plastic dinner plates. He held a piece of paper covered with new work assignments by his side. After watching the way several women had been whispering behind the men's backs, he'd decided to change things up. He didn't want any factions to start to develop. Maintaining order was hard enough without active dissent.

pockets. If they'd been alone, he would have slapped the smirk off of her face.

"It does make sense to create some kind of council," Ivan said. "Up until now, you haven't really asked what everyone wants to do, you've just told us."

"Because I'm guided by God," Elijah said.

"Even so, I doubt He's interested in the day-to-day operations at one of His *many* churches," Melinda said.

"Maybe we should discuss this privately," Elijah said.

"Matters involving the community should be discussed as a group. I realize we can't have forty people trying to agree on everything, which is why we should vote for council members. We could choose five people to represent the community."

"And I suppose you will be one of the five?"

"Only if elected."

"I'll need to pray about it," he said. "In the meantime, everyone, please try to have a good evening. Melinda, come walk with me so we can discuss details of your council idea."

He stalked toward his office and waited until Melinda was inside before closing the door.

"How dare you question me in front of everyone," he said. "You're here because I allow you to stay. But maybe you're ready to leave. Maybe you should go back to your house and fend for yourself there."

"How dare I? How dare you!" Her face flushed. "You treat us like slaves and run this place like a dictatorship."

"What's happening to you? You were never this belligerent."

"Nothing's wrong with me, but something's not right with this community. Everyone's too afraid to speak up. Several people have gone missing and when we ask you where they went, you tell us they left the community."

"Because they have. Not everyone chooses to stay. If you're not happy here, no one will stop you from leaving. I can't understand what your problem is. You've been here since the bombs dropped. Why the sudden change?"

"I've felt this way since you assigned everyone jobs."

"Yet you did nothing to stop me then."

"Because I didn't want to make waves."

"But you do now. Why?" He took a step toward her, enjoying the way she cowered away. "Is this coming from that woman?"

"What woman?"

"The one whose daughter is cavorting with your son."

"Liz?"

"How do you know her name?"

"Adam told me."

"Have you spoken with her?"

"Never."

"But Adam has."

"Not that I know of."

"I should remove him from water duty or at least send another man with him. These women, running around unsupervised by a husband, it's not right. They will poison your mind with falsehoods about us. Are you not happy here? Do I not feed you?"

"You starved us."

"I regret that," he lied. "I should have been more lenient."

"It's not your place to judge us."

"Isn't it?" he asked. "Who else will keep the community from falling into chaos? Do you want to be like the people in the cities? Scurrying like rats for a bite of rotting bread?"

"How do you know what's happening in the cities?"

"I've sent men to look for others. People who can join us and help support the community."

"Where will they live?"

"In the abandoned houses."

"Those belong to other people."

"Who may or may not choose to come back," he said. "You need to start trusting me. I've done nothing to deserve your attack."

"I didn't attack you."

He pressed his lips together. His hands flinched as he momentarily fantasized about wrapping them around her neck. Was this what Samson felt when he'd realized Delilah's betrayal?

"I need time to think, and to pray about the future of our community," he said. "Please close the door when you leave."

For a moment, she didn't move. He narrowed his gaze, which spurred her into motion.

After she'd left, he swiped a pile of books off of his desk. As they clattered to the ground, he realized the issue wasn't with Melinda. She'd been a good servant to the community until her son had been tempted by Sierra. She was the root of this evil swirling through Melinda's mind.

If he got rid of Sierra and her mother permanently, he could restore order to the group. But how? Attacking their home had resulted in two deaths already. No, he couldn't make a stand there. They'd have the advantage. But he had another idea. A perfect plan to end the discord within his flock.

14

Liz cracked open the door to the shipping area. Rather than risk shining a flashlight into the darkness, she paused. She strained to listen for any indication of people inside. Nothing moved. The absolute stillness did little to calm her nerves, but at least they hadn't been ambushed. They'd be in and out before anyone in the area realized they were there.

"Ten minutes," she whispered.

"Yeah," the guys responded.

She flicked on a tiny flashlight. Its dim glow illuminated a two-foot-wide path. She used it to scan the mostly empty shelves in the storage area. Apparently they didn't keep much back stock. The few items left included clothes, dumbbells, and Christmas decorations. Nothing edible.

As she headed toward a pair of doors, she glanced over her shoulder. Harvey's jaw tightened. His lips formed a thin line. The hand gripping his pistol clenched, but his finger didn't move from the side.

She pushed through the swinging doors and stepped into a disaster zone. The electronics section contained shattered DVD cases. Smashed TVs were strewn across the floor. Headphones with dangling wires formed tangled tentacles of useless technology. Books and magazines sat in shredded heaps.

Moving forward, she kicked a copy of a popular self-help book out of the way. All that psycho-babble wouldn't do much good these days. People would either man up and learn to live in the new world, or die. At first she'd been hesitant to accept her new reality, but as each day melted into the next, she'd come to the realization that no one was going to help her. She had to learn to help herself.

Across the aisle, Franklin and Burt disappeared into a section of toppled furniture. Apparently no one was interested in redecorating.

She headed toward the baby section. Strollers lay on their sides. Baby clothing was tossed all over the aisles. She found the baby food section. Two jars of mashed peas lay on their sides. She picked one up and inspected it. The plastic jar and seal were intact. It wasn't much, but it gave her a shot of hope.

"Let's see what else we can get," she whispered.

"Okay."

As she and Harvey piled formula and jars of food into a bag, she smiled. If people had overlooked this area, they might have missed other items in the store. Hopefully Franklin and Bert were having some luck too.

After gathering two bags' worth of food, she motioned toward the grocery section. She passed row after row of stripped-bare shelves. Six rows back, she finally found a lone can of olives. It lay on its side underneath the bottom shelf. If she hadn't been paying close attention, she would have missed it.

She stuffed it into a bag before walking to the next aisle. She meticulously searched every shelf, adding several cans of Spam, a jar of pickled pig's feet, and a half-torn-open bag of black-eyed peas. It wasn't the biggest grocery haul, but it was better than nothing.

"It's been ten minutes," Harvey whispered. "Let's head back."

"You lead."

He nodded and took point. As they made their way back toward the loading docks, she strained to pick up Franklin and Burt's location. She didn't hear their footsteps. Maybe they were already outside?

When they reached the set of double doors, she

grabbed the back of Harvey's shirt and turned off the flashlight.

"Something feels off."

"I feel it too," he murmured.

"Maybe we should go out the front and circle around."

"If we change the plan, the others might not know it's us and they'll shoot."

"Good point," she said. "What about going in through a different door? If someone else is on the other side, we'll at least have a surprise advantage."

A loud metallic bang reverberated from the loading docks.

Harvey's eyes went wide. He pointed down the wall toward another set of doors they'd spotted on the way in. She took the lead and headed for the other exit.

When she pushed on the door, it didn't budge. She glanced at Harvey, who shrugged. Without light, she couldn't figure out why it wasn't opening. She felt along the door and found a large bolt at the top. As she pulled down, nothing happened, but when she pushed up, the door popped free and swung open.

Flashlights blinded her. She held up an arm to block the light. With her gun hand, she pointed toward the dark shadows behind the light.

"Don't shoot!" Franklin said. He directed his

flashlight at the ground. Burt flicked his off. "What the hell are you guys doing over here?"

"We heard a bang so we decided to come this way instead," Harvey said.

"If you were trying for a tactical advantage, you failed," Franklin said.

"What was that noise?" she asked.

"Burt didn't want to use the lights and ran into a trash can. The lid fell off," Franklin said.

"Did you guys find anything useful?"

"A couple of bags of beef jerky, some astronaut ice cream, and a couple of cases of freeze-dried camping food," Burt said.

"What about survival kits?" she asked. "Sometimes they have those three-day or even thirty-day kits."

"We found a three-day, but it only had enough calories to keep one person barely alive. I don't know why they keep the calorie counts so low," Burt said.

"No thirty-day kits?"

"No."

"We found some baby food and some canned stuff. Not much," she said. "Should we check Walmart next?"

"Yeah."

After stowing the new food supply, they drove toward Walmart. Situated between both entrances to the store, a huge bonfire lit up the night. Trucks formed a large circle around the fire. Men and women stood around the fire with guns in one hand, beer in the other. At a quick glance, she guessed there were at least fifty people.

"Turn around," she said.

"Yep." Burt made a U-turn in the middle of the road and headed back toward the movie theater.

"What about that office building?" Harvey asked.

"Good call," she said. "Go around back. I don't think those guys saw us, but just in case, we should hide the truck again."

"What are we looking for?" Franklin asked.

"Vending machines. A break room. People's desks. Look for anything edible. We didn't get nearly enough food from Target. We need more. A lot more," she said.

"Ten-minute time limit?" Harvey asked.

"I don't think we'll be able to search the whole building in ten minutes, so let's start with the top floor and assess after every floor. We need to move fast," she said.

"Are you sure this is a good idea?" Harvey asked. "I think we should head back."

"We don't have enough food yet."

"I know, but we're also still alive. We could get trapped up there if other people show up."

"I wouldn't have guessed that since you're so active in our group."

"You're nice people, not assholes." He shrugged. "I guess I got lucky in that regard."

"I can't carry anything else." Franklin walked up. "Let's drop everything off and finish off the building."

After unloading their haul, they returned to clean out the first floor. Franklin and Burt climbed into the truck bed.

"Let's go home." Liz hopped into the passenger seat.

The trip back to the cabins took well over an hour. They'd circled around Portola Hills so they wouldn't run into the clubhouse group again.

On the drive back, Liz strategized how best to retain as much food as possible. Since her family didn't have anything left, it shouldn't be too hard to convince the others to give her the lion's share of their haul. At least she hoped it wouldn't be. But there were plenty of stubborn women in their community, so she spent the rest of the trip mentally preparing for a fight.

SIERRA DRAGGED her feet as she headed toward the

creek for her fifth water run for the day. Losing their food supply was all her fault. If she hadn't been so eager to hang out with other people, the preacher and his weird family would never have discovered the cabin. She kept messing up and didn't know how she could ever make it up to her family. They'd probably hate her forever.

She shuddered to think about how disappointed her dad would be when he got home. He'd spent years stockpiling supplies. And in one night, her carelessness had cost them everything. Now they had nothing to eat. Her mom was out risking her life to get more food. What if she got killed? What would she do? She wasn't prepared to take care of Kyle.

Another question nagged at the edge of her mind. Was Adam involved in the theft? She'd told him about their food supply. Maybe not specifics, but he had to know they were well off if she had enough to share. Was he part of this? Did he tell the preacher about the cans she'd given him? Had he betrayed her trust?

She hated the world they were living in. Ever since the bombings, she didn't know who she could trust. In the old world, most people were kind and good. But now… now it was a different world. A broken world. One in which she couldn't trust anyone or anything.

From now on, she'd have to be much more careful

about who she talked to, and about what she said. Giving information away would only hurt her in the long run.

She set one of the buckets on a rock next to the creek. She took the other into the rushing water and scooped up as much as she could carry. As she walked back toward the empty bucket, footsteps sounded on the path. She quickly set the bucket down and spun around. Adam slowly walked toward her. He carried a bucket in each hand.

"They put you on water detail too?" she asked.

"Yeah."

"You look like crap."

"I feel like crap." He flipped a bucket over and sat on it. "I need to rest for a minute."

"Are you sick?"

"No. Just hungry. I don't have any energy left."

"I thought you'd be feasting today," she said with a heap of sarcasm.

"Why would you think that?"

"Don't play dumb."

"What are you talking about?" he asked warily.

"Last night a bunch of men stole all of our food."

"What?"

"Yeah. Know anything about it?" She put her hands on her hips and glared.

"No, but…"

"What?"

"I heard there was a feast at the church last night. My mom and I weren't allowed to eat dinner last night or this morning. And I've been on bucket detail all day."

"I've been walking back and forth to the stream for an hour and I didn't see you here," she challenged. "And this is our stream. You shouldn't even be here."

"Why are you so pissed?"

"Because you told them." Her voice cracked. "How could you do that to me? I thought we were friends."

"I didn't tell them anything. I didn't even tell my mom about the cans you gave me."

"I don't believe you. Why was the preacher mad at your mom?"

"I don't know. I can't believe you think I told them. Why would I do that? We're friends. At least, I thought we were."

"The feast you mentioned—that was *our* food. They stole it."

He hung his head and covered his face with his hands.

"Don't lie to me," she snapped.

"I'm not lying. I didn't tell anyone, and I didn't know they were going to steal your food."

"Well they did, and now—" She stopped short.

She wasn't going to tell him a damn thing about her mom heading off to find more. If the preacher found out she and Kyle were alone, there was no telling what he might do.

"I'm sorry. I hate him. He's evil. I can't understand why no one else sees it. I think my mom does, but every time I try to talk to her about it, she tells me to be quiet. She's afraid someone will overhear us. The place was nice at first, but it's getting weirder by the day. He's setting up all kinds of rules, and if you break them, there's hell to pay."

"What kind of hell?" she asked.

"He's withholding food, even water sometimes. He's running the group like a king. Like we're his servants or something. It's weird. I want to leave, but my mom says we don't have anywhere else to go. I'd be happy to be homeless at this point if it means getting away from him."

"So you really didn't tell him?"

"No." His blue eyes reflected the pale gray sky. "I'd never betray you like that. I don't tell him anything. Not that I have anything to hide, but if I did, I sure as hell wouldn't talk to him."

The dejected tone of his voice pulled at her heart. The preacher victimized him just as much as he'd victimized her family. She struggled against the urge to comfort him. Maybe this was all an act to get closer to her. Although he seemed sincere, she was hesitant to trust him.

"Have you asked your mom about going back to your house in Coto?" she asked.

"Multiple times. She always tells me it's not an option."

"Maybe the fact that he's starving you guys will help her change her mind."

"I don't know. She thinks there's strength in numbers."

"Only if they're going to take care of each other."

"True."

"You should talk to her again. Tell her that you can't stay there anymore."

"I'll try. At this point I'd rather go home and try to defend my house than stay here." He stood and grabbed his buckets. "I need to get back before they notice I've been gone longer than normal."

"I'm sorry you're trapped."

"Me too."

After he filled the buckets, he headed back down the trail toward the preacher's compound. As much as she wanted to harden her heart against him, she couldn't. He'd never done anything to make her question his friendship. He didn't seem like the kind of person who could lie right to your face without flinching. The preacher certainly could, but not Adam.

So maybe her judgment wasn't as bad as she'd thought. When she'd first met the preacher, she hadn't liked him. He had the gross, slimy vibe of a reptile. If only she'd listened to her gut.

Going forward, she'd pay more attention to that inner voice that told her something wasn't right. She only wished she'd listened when she'd met the preacher. She could have avoided so much trouble.

As she filled the buckets, she vowed to do better. She needed to help her mom. She'd been working so hard and looked totally exhausted every day. Even though her dad would be back in a few days, she knew it wouldn't change much. There were too many tasks and not enough people to complete them.

Before the bombs, she'd enjoyed the occasional afternoon nap between classes. Back then, she hadn't thought twice about that little bit of freedom. Now she'd give anything to be able to go back to that simpler time. Would she ever be able to take a nap again? Probably not, so she might as well get used to it.

15

Luke winced as each step sent a spark of pain down his leg. Blood saturated the bandage. He needed to replace it and suck down a pain pill—or ten. He'd briefly considered attempting to infiltrate the hospital, but after hearing about its condition from the kids, he knew it would be a lost cause.

He and Boyd had been following Mason and Noah's chalk line for the better part of an hour. As far as Luke could tell, they were still headed south. They hadn't encountered the kids, or anyone else, but he hadn't relaxed his guard. He kept the flashlight in his left hand, while his right hand rested on the butt of his gun.

Pale light streamed down from open gutters every few hundred feet. He figured they'd entered a residential neighborhood, but hadn't risked a peek. He didn't want to go out until after dark. The throbbing in his leg wasn't a good sign. He doubted he'd be able to outrun any attackers. Once they got topside, he needed to check for infection. Based on feel alone, it wasn't looking good.

"We've got maybe an hour or so before sundown," Luke said. "We need to find a place to stay tonight."

"Not down here," Boyd said.

"Definitely not. If a flood came tearing through here in the middle of the night, we'd be screwed. Also, I think we should start looking for antibiotics."

"Is the leg bothering you?"

"Yeah."

"How bad?"

"If I had to outrun an eighty-year-old in a wheelchair, I'd be in trouble."

"Maybe we need a saw."

"A saw?"

"In case we have to chop it off."

Luke glanced back at Boyd, who was grinning like the Cheshire cat.

"You come near me with a saw and I'll remove one of *your* appendages," Luke said.

"I'd give up a hand. You know, so I don't have to wash dishes anymore. The wife's always getting on me about how I do the dishes. *They're not clean enough*," he said in a high-pitched tone. "*There's stuff stuck to the plate.*"

"I'd be on your ass about it too if there was crap on the plate."

"Ninny."

Luke shook his head and smiled.

"When we get to the next manhole, let's push it up and take a peek," Boyd said. "If we need to find antibiotics, it would be better to search while there's still some daylight. Flashlights at night are a dead giveaway."

"Good point."

"I'm not just a pretty face," Boyd said. "Hopefully we'll be able to find a pharmacy."

"I doubt there are any that haven't been ransacked."

"Worst case scenario, we look for a pet store."

"A pet store? Why?"

"Fish antibiotics. We had a betta fish for a few years. Mr. Snuggles."

"Seriously?"

"I didn't name him. I let my daughter Molly pick it. Anyway, one day the poor guy wasn't looking so hot so I went to the pet store. They had a bunch of antibiotics. Penicillin, tetracycline, erythromycin, sulfa. I couldn't believe it. If we can find some, we could try that."

"Do you think it's safe?" Luke asked.

"I sure as hell wouldn't try it in normal circumstances, but we're not in a normal situation. Sure, I'd love to be able to walk into a doctor's office and get the real deal, but that won't be happening any time soon."

"I don't know. I've never heard of this before."

"Hopefully we won't have to resort to that," Boyd said. "Let's get out of this damn tunnel and go look for a pharmacy."

Luke pointed the flashlight into the dark tunnel. He continued walking until he reached a series of metal rungs in the wall. After confirming they led to a manhole, he handed the flashlight to Boyd.

"I'll go up first. Keep the light on the cover. Get ready to turn it off as soon as I get the thing open."

"Roger."

Luke's leg burned as he climbed to the top. As he steadied himself with one hand, he used the other to push up on the manhole. It didn't budge.

"You want me to come up?" Boyd asked.

"Give me another minute."

Luke leaned forward and climbed two more steps. With his shoulder pressed up against the manhole, he used his good leg as leverage to force the cover up a fraction of an inch.

"You got it," Boyd called. "Keep pushing."

As he heaved with all of his strength, the manhole ripped free of whatever had been holding it in place. A cascade of dirt and grime tumbled down the hole.

"Fuck. Right in the eye," Boyd yelled.

"Shh!"

"Easy for you to say. You don't have slime in your fucking eye."

"Wash it out while I look around."

Luke pushed the manhole off to one side. He poked his head up like a gopher. From the middle of an intersection, he spotted houses on one side and a strip mall on the other. Not bad. Maybe they could find a pharmacy here.

After scanning for threats, Luke pulled himself up out of the hole.

"It's clear. Let's move before someone sees us."

"Coming."

When Boyd reached the surface, Luke stifled a laugh. Muck from around the manhole dribbled down his cheeks. Unidentifiable debris littered his hair, and a shriveled candy wrapper clung to the top of his head.

"What?" Boyd demanded.

"You look like a dumpster-diving raccoon."

"Asshole." Boyd flailed his hands across his face and hair, trying to push the rest of the gunk off.

"It's gone. Let's check out the shopping center."

"Why's it so quiet here?" Boyd asked.

"I don't know."

He made a good point. He'd expected to run into at least one or two people. The sun hung low on the horizon, but it hadn't completely set yet. Why was the neighborhood so quiet?

"Do you smell that?" Boyd asked.

"Yeah, smells like death."

"We should get face masks too if we can find them."

"Let's try that dollar store."

"They won't have antibiotics."

"No, but sometimes they have aspirin and medical supplies. I don't mind strapping tampons to my leg, but if I have the choice, I'd prefer maxi pads. More absorbent."

"You're killing me with your feminine hygiene talk."

"But it works."

"True."

As Luke approached the front of the dollar store, he signaled to Boyd to be quiet. He peeked around the corner through a glass window into the store. Toppled shelves lay at forty-five degree angles against the wall. Fall-themed knickknacks were strewn across the floor. A headless ceramic turkey lay shattered next to a cash wrap. Cardboard boxes with charred edges were piled in the center of the store, as if the looters had tried to set the whole place on fire.

"Damn," Boyd said.

"As far as I can tell, it's clear. Let's see what we can find. Don't turn your back to the front of the store and keep the rear exits in mind, just in case."

Boyd nodded and stepped over the window seal. Luke followed, crunching through shards of shattered glass. Most of the shelves were empty. He walked through a pile of empty plastic packages. They'd been ripped open, their contents stolen.

He found the medical supply section. A lone bottle of talcum powder lay on its side. Bandages were scattered across the floor. No point in taking those. They definitely weren't sanitary anymore.

After searching through several other aisles, he crossed to the other side of the store where Boyd poked through a pile of books.

"Find anything?" Luke asked.

"Some coloring books, crayons."

"We could use those to make candles."

"We've got flashlights. I sure as hell don't want to have to carry more than what I've already got," Boyd said.

"I hear you. Just thinking out loud."

"We're not that far from my house. Maybe ten miles. We should be able to make it there by tomorrow. I only want to carry what I already have, unless it's something really good. What did you find?"

"Nothing. It's been stripped clean."

"Should we hunker down here for the night? I doubt anyone would try to search this place after dark. Everyone in the area probably knows it's empty. Hell, they might have stockpiles in their houses."

"Are you suggesting we break into people's houses and look around?" Luke asked.

"No. But I smell a lot of death. We could try to look through any empty houses. See if they left antibiotics behind."

"Breaking into someone's house to steal their stuff doesn't feel right."

"Even if they're dead?" Boyd asked.

"What makes you think we're going to find a bunch of dead people?"

"You don't get that kind of stench unless there are a lot of dead bodies around."

"How would you know?"

"When I was a kid, we lived on the other side of a mortuary. I could always tell when they were doing cremations. The scent of burning flesh is about as distinctive a smell as you can get. I know what death smells like, and it's all around us. I wouldn't be surprised if the whole neighborhood had been slaughtered."

"By who?"

"Who knows? Gangs. Criminals. By now the prisons have probably run out of food. They might have released the prisoners."

"God, I hope not."

"Me too."

"I guess we could look around and see if any of the houses are vacant."

"Let me see your leg," Boyd said.

Luke peeled the bandage back. Angry red lines radiated out from the wound. Puffy skin surrounded it while a trickle of white puss oozed from the flesh.

"That's not good. Is it hot?" Boyd asked.

Luke gently placed his fingers over the skin. "Yep."

"Then we need to get antibiotics. It already looks like you might have a blood infection. If we don't get medicine into you as soon as possible, you won't make it home to your family. Hell, you might not even make it to my house."

"Thanks for cheering me up."

"Anytime. Let's slap a tampon on that and get moving. The longer we wait, the worse it will get. I know you're hung up on the ethics of taking antibiotics from people, but without them you're going to die."

"I don't want to rob anyone."

"We'll only take what we can find in empty houses. And if we don't find anything, we'll look for a fish store. Let's go, Mr. Snuggles."

"Don't even think about giving me that nickname."

Boyd laughed. Luke reached into his pack and grabbed a tampon and some tape. After covering the wound and securing the makeshift bandage, he headed toward the front of the store. Taking supplies from other people didn't sit right with him, but Boyd had a point. If he didn't get antibiotics soon, he wouldn't be around to debate ethics in a post-apocalyptic world.

LUKE PULLED a white bandana out of his pack and tied it across his face to cover his mouth and nose. The stench of decaying corpses made their voyage through the storm drains smell like a rose garden in comparison. He hopped a white picket fence in the backyard of the third house on the block. So far they'd found four dead and no antibiotics. He wasn't sure what would be worse: Finding more dead bodies, or running into a living threat.

"Hopefully this one's the ticket," Boyd whispered.

"God willing."

Luke ran to the back porch and pressed his back against the wall. He stood still, listening for several minutes. The absolute silence grated on his nerves. Was everyone dead? Had some group systematically wiped out every family on the block?

As he turned to peer into a rear window, he held his breath and hoped he wouldn't find himself staring down the barrel of a gun.

The bedroom contained a set of dressers, a bed, and a closet. Everything looked normal. But he'd seen that before in the previous homes, at least in the bedrooms. The bathrooms and kitchens had been completely ransacked. Nothing was left. Not even a single Band-Aid. But he wasn't ready to give up hope. He only needed one bottle of medicine.

"Let's check the living room," Luke whispered.

Boyd nodded and followed him to a sliding glass door at the rear of the house. A quick glance revealed another nightmarish scene. An older man lay sprawled in a recliner. The top part of his head had become a liquid halo of flesh and bone on the wall. His jaw hung open and he regarded the ceiling with opaque eyes.

Across the room, a woman slumped across the couch. A TV remote lay at her feet, as if she'd been watching it when the killers had entered. The center of her chest bore a large red hole rimmed with congealed blood. A second gunshot had ripped through her temple.

Bile roared up Luke's throat. He stumbled to the kitchen and hurled into the sink. The gore didn't bother him. He'd seen far worse as a SEAL. But to think this could be his family's fate too cut him to the core. He'd spoken to Liz several days earlier, but that didn't mean a damn thing. Life could be ripped away in an instant. All it took was one desperate man to destroy a family.

"You okay?" Boyd asked.

"Yeah."

Luke turned on the faucet. Nothing flowed. He grabbed a roll of paper towels from the counter. As he wiped his face, his stomach clenched. He fought a second wave of nausea. Sweat broke out on his forehead.

"You don't look so good. Maybe you should sit down."

"We have to clear the house first."

"Whoever did this is long gone."

"I want to be sure," Luke said.

"I'll lead."

Luke nodded. He didn't mind letting Boyd take over. The man had proved to be more than capable of clearing a room. The longer they worked together, the more they were becoming a team.

After checking all the bedrooms, including the closets, they swept the bathroom. The medicine cabinet hung open. It was as empty as the rest.

"You know those night stands we saw in the master bedroom?"

"Yeah."

"We haven't been searching those," Boyd said.

"You think they might have meds stashed away in them?"

"Maybe. My grandparents had medicine in theirs. I got into it once when I was a kid. Took an entire bottle of blood pressure pills. They had to take me to the hospital and pump my stomach. I was unconscious for two days."

"That explains a lot."

"Funny," Boyd said dryly. "They found me before the brain damage kicked in."

"I don't know. Lack of oxygen fries those brain cells."

"Remind me again, why am I helping you?"

"Because I'm Mr. Snuggles."

Boyd doubled over laughing. When he finally straightened, he wiped tears from his eyes. "God, I needed that."

"Let's find some medicine."

Luke headed into the master bedroom. The first

drawer contained a worn copy of *Pride and Prejudice*. He closed it.

When he opened the second drawer, he spotted two pill bottles. He turned up the label on the first one. Lipitor. That wasn't going to help.

He twisted the second bottle around. His heart sank.

"Well, the good news is that I found some. The bad news is that I'm allergic to it."

"What is it?"

"Penicillin."

"I'm not allergic. Mind if I hang onto it? Antibiotics will be a hot commodity until they get the lights back on."

"Take it." He handed the bottle to Boyd.

"Should we go back and check the other bedrooms?"

"In the other houses?"

"Maybe we missed something."

"It couldn't hurt," Luke said.

They returned to the previous houses and searched. After coming up empty, they approached the fourth house.

"You hear anything?" Boyd whispered.

"No. You?"

"No."

"Let's do this."

Luke walked through the shattered sliding glass door. Unlike the other houses, this one wasn't full of corpses. On high alert, Luke headed down the hall. He walked slowly, cringing as warped floorboards creaked. So much for stealth.

One of the doors in the hallway was closed. He approached the room. As he reached for the doorknob, he changed the grip on his gun to stabilize it. He turned the doorknob and pushed it open. A pink cradle sat in one corner, a rocking chair in the other. Several bags of diapers and a huge pile of clean washcloths were stacked on a bookshelf alongside a copy of *What to Expect When You're Expecting.*

He glanced back at Boyd who was fixated on the cradle. He was probably thinking the same thing, *please don't let there be a baby in it.*

He swallowed the lump in his throat and plodded through thick brown carpet. A heaped blanket lay inside the cradle. He stopped breathing. He reached for the blanket.

It moved.

He jumped back, slamming into Boyd.

"Did you see that?" Luke asked.

"Please tell me I'm hallucinating."

Luke stepped forward and grabbed the edge of the blanket. As he peeled it back, a cat leapt out.

"Shit!"

The tabby cat raced between Boyd's legs and ran out into the hall.

"A damn cat?" Boyd said, breathlessly.

"I thought I was going to have a heart attack."

"You and me both. Maybe we should have taken the Lipitor."

"I'm tempted to go back for it after that."

"At least it wasn't a baby."

"Thank God."

"How long has that cat been in here?" Boyd asked.

"The window's open and there's a hole in the screen. She's probably been coming in and out since the apocalypse. Let's check the rest of the house."

"If anyone was in here, they would have shot us by now with all the noise we've been making."

"Good point. But let's check anyway."

After clearing the rest of the house, they headed back toward the living room. The cat stood in the middle of the kitchen next to an empty bowl.

"She must live here," Boyd said.

"Let's see if we can find something for her to eat."

Most of the cupboards were bare, but he managed to find a couple of cans on the top shelf. After using a manual can opener, he dumped the slippery contents into the bowl. The cat gorged on the food.

"We should find him some water too," Luke said.

"I'll check the garage. Sometimes people keep cases of bottled water in there."

While Boyd went to search, Luke rummaged through the rest of the shelves. He found a half-eaten package of saltine crackers and several cans of green beans. He cracked open a can and drained the water into the cat's bowl. The cat meowed and brushed her head against Luke's leg.

"I found a couple of bottles of water," Boyd said as he set the bottles on the counter.

"I've got beans. We should eat them since they're relatively heavy."

"Hang on, I found something else in the garage." Boyd disappeared for a minute before returning with several cans. "Chili con carne."

"Oh hell yeah."

"We can even eat out of bowls like civilized people."

"Civilized..." Luke shook his head. "Can you believe all of this? I still feel like I'm in some kind of nightmare."

"I've been trying to wake up for almost two weeks."

"How could this have happened in America?"

"We got complacent. Too many countries have nukes. And it might not have even been a single country. It could have been a rogue organization like

ISIS. You wouldn't believe how many nukes have gone missing from Russia over the years."

"I believe it," Luke said. "All it takes is one to start a war."

"I wish we had more information about what's going on. I never thought I'd miss the news as much as I do. Hell, I'd even take fake news over no news."

"I don't know if I'd go that far."

"You're right. I miss the old news anchors who would just tell us the facts without adding their opinions into everything."

"The good old days," Luke said with a nod.

As they dished out the chili, they fell into a comfortable silence. Luke devoured two cans before calling it quits.

"Should we stay here tonight?"

"We could try it. Whoever lives here could come back, but I doubt it," Boyd said.

"They could be anywhere."

"Maybe they're not even in the country. If they were on vacation when everything happened, they'd be stranded overseas."

"I'm glad I was still in California," Luke said. "It's been hell trying to get this far. I can't even imagine trying to navigate life in another country."

"I can take first watch."

"Great. All that chili put me into a stupor."

"Just be sure to crack a window. You don't want to gas us in the middle of the night."

Luke laughed. "I'll be in the master bedroom. Might as well sleep in a bed while I can."

"Sounds good.

Boyd sat in a chair next to the sliding glass door. From his position, he had a clear shot at all of the doors including the one from the garage into the kitchen.

Luke headed into the master bedroom. He pulled the top drawer in the night stand out and dug through its contents. A bottle of amoxicillin rolled toward the front of the drawer. Perfect!

After popping two pills, he kicked off his boots and flopped face down on the bed. He was asleep before his head hit the pillow.

Hours later, he woke to the sound of breaking glass.

16

Elijah strolled up and down the line of five men who stood at attention in front of the gun shed. Turner leaned against the shed door.

"What has Turner told you about our community?" Elijah asked.

"You're a group of God-fearing men who are preparing for the end of days," Gunther said. At six foot three inches, he towered over the others. Elijah hated having to strain his neck to look up at him, but the man was a solid wall of muscle, perfect for enforcing Elijah's rules.

"What else did he say?" Elijah asked.

"That you've been having problems with some woman and her brats," Steve said. He was short and stocky. A glint of darkness shimmered in his beady eyes. Elijah would have to keep a close eye on him. He could either prove to be a great asset, or a loose cannon.

"Yes. The woman and her kids live in a cabin over the hill and past a stream. They are a huge threat to our community and I want them brought to one of the empty houses. They need to be taught… *manners.*"

"You want us to kidnap them?" Jim asked. The third man wasn't nearly as big as the other two, but he sported wiry muscles in his arms. He could probably snap a man's neck with little effort. However, his hesitation wasn't welcome.

"You're here on a trial basis," Elijah said. "If you're not comfortable with keeping our community safe from all threats, you're welcome to leave at any time. In order to remain with the group, you must complete this mission. We're only taking five recruits right now. I trust Turner's judgment. He wouldn't have chosen you if he didn't believe in your skills, and I wouldn't ask you to capture these people if they weren't actively trying to destroy everything I've worked to build."

He stopped to assess their expressions. The skepticism in Jim's expression slowly faded. Good. Elijah didn't want to have to kill him, but he wasn't about to let anyone walk away from the community again. Not

her brats. Once he had them, he'd find a way to discreetly get rid of them. Trying to get them to see his point of view was a worthless endeavor. If anything, letting them linger around the community would help spread their cancerous ideas. The sooner he could be rid of them, the better.

Sierra woke with a start. The phantom sound of bells ringing echoed through her head. Had it been another nightmare, or had she really heard the bells from the tripwires?

She slipped out of bed and wrapped a robe around herself. She crossed the loft to where her brother slept. Unless a horde of zombies came tearing through the house, he wouldn't wake up. She envied his ability to sleep like the dead.

As she descended the stairs, she listened intently.

There. Bells. This time she definitely heard them. And they were closer.

For a split second, she wondered if it could be her mom. But, no. She'd never set off the tripwires. It had to be someone else. Maybe the preacher's men back to steal from them again. Not that they had anything left to steal.

"Kyle," she yelled. "Get up."

He didn't move. Damn him.

She hurried toward the front door to check the two by four barricade. The back door was also locked and barricaded.

Back at the front window, she peeled the curtain back an inch. Darkness pressed in from outside. Without a single light, she could only make out the slight change in darkness between the open space and the tree line. Her eyes had already adjusted to the darkness because they kept every light in the house off during the night. Even so, she couldn't see a damn thing.

She grabbed a rifle from the gun rack and chambered a round. She ejected the magazine and checked to be sure it was full before slamming it home.

She walked to a window on the side of the house which faced the shed. If they were coming back to steal more food, the joke would be on them. They'd already taken everything. Assholes.

Maybe she was totally overreacting and it was just an animal. She returned to the front and checked outside. Nothing moved as far as she could tell.

Wait. What was that?

She squinted. Her mom had taken the night vision goggles with her. Too bad, because they would have been a huge help right now.

Her breath came out in shallow bursts. A minute

passed. Then another. The tension in her spine relaxed slightly. It had probably been an animal.

After setting the rifle down, she plopped down in a chair at the kitchen table. She lowered her face to her hands. Was life always going to be like this now? Would she always be on edge, jumping at the slightest noise or shadow?

Although she hadn't been getting along with her mom, she missed her. She'd promised she'd be home by sunrise. Without a watch or any way of telling time, she had to read the color of the sky and guess at the time. Probably close to five a.m. Two hours until sunrise.

She poured a glass of water to quench her suddenly parched throat. Upstairs, Kyle stirred. His footsteps moved across the ceiling before reaching the ladder. He met her in the kitchen.

"What are you doing up?" he asked.

"I thought I heard something."

"What?"

"The bells."

"I didn't hear anything."

"An airplane could buzz the house and you wouldn't hear it," she said.

"I'd wake up for an airplane. I haven't heard one in weeks. Do you think we'll ever be able to fly again?"

"I don't know."

"Do you think the power will come back on?"

"I don't know."

"What about—"

"Stop asking me shit I don't know," she snapped.

"Why are you such a bitch all the time?"

"Because I want my life back. I never thought it would end up like this. I thought I'd go to school, get a degree, get married, have kids, have a life. Now none of that's ever going to happen."

"You really believe that?" he asked softly.

"Yes!"

"I don't. I think the power's going to come back on and that everything will go back to normal."

"Enjoy your delusion." She couldn't stop herself. His Pollyanna-like view of the future enraged her. He couldn't be more wrong. Life was over and no one seemed to get it.

"I can't wait for Mom to get home," he said. "Or Dad."

"I miss Dad too."

"He should be here soon."

"I hope so."

"I'm going back to bed." As he turned to leave, something thumped against the back door. "Did you hear that?" he whispered.

"Go hide in the bathroom." When he didn't immediately move, she shoved him. "Now!"

As she ran toward the discarded rifle, one of the back windows shattered. A hail of glass crashed to the floor a split second before two men vaulted into the cabin. She screamed and grabbed the rifle.

She spun toward them and managed to get off one wild shot before a man shoved her against the wall and ripped the rifle out of her hands. Before she could react, he slapped her across the face.

"Stop fucking moving or we'll hurt you," he growled.

She thrashed and struggled to no avail. He turned her around and slammed her against the wall hard enough to make her teeth cut her lip and draw blood. He put something around her wrists and yanked it so tight it cut into her skin. She kicked backward at his knee, but only grazed it. He slammed the butt of his gun into the middle of her back. She screamed as pain flared out in every direction.

"Check the bathroom," the second man said.

"No!"

"Where's your mother?" the first man demanded.

"Fuck you."

When he backhanded her, she took a second to recover before spitting in his face. He laughed and wiped it away.

"Did Mommy run off and leave you all alone?"

"She'll be here any minute and she's going to kill you all," Sierra lied. If only it was true.

When the second man dragged Kyle out of the bathroom, her heart sank. She hadn't been able to do a damn thing to protect him. Sure, he was a little brat most of the time, but he was still her brother. She'd completely failed him. She'd completely failed her family. Again.

The man shoved Kyle against the wall. They stood shoulder to shoulder in silence.

"Check upstairs," the first man said.

After climbing the stairs, the man stomped around. Furniture scraped across the floor. Pillows flew over the railing to land on the bottom floor.

"No sign of her," the man called down.

"Let's wait and see if she comes back. Maybe she's out on patrol."

"I'll let the others know."

Others? The hair on the back of her neck stood on end. There were more of them? How many? What if her mom did show up right now? She'd be totally outnumbered and outgunned.

And all of this—all of it—was Sierra's fault. Her careless mistake in talking to the preacher's people had started them down a path ultimately leading to this moment.

Ten minutes passed. Then thirty. Then an hour. Outside, the sky brightened from black to a dull gray.

"Sunrise is coming," the first man said. "We need to head back."

"I'll get the boy. You take her."

"If you give me any problems, I'll shoot you and leave you on the front porch for your mom to find," the first man said. "Got it?"

"Yes."

"Good. Now move your ass."

He shoved her toward the back door and continued to shove her all the way through the forest. She wasn't surprised in the least to find herself being herded toward the preacher's compound.

A dull sunrise cast shadows over the land. Instead of walking toward the church, they corralled her toward a house about a half mile deeper into the canyon. Once inside, they sat her and Kyle down in wooden chairs at a kitchen table. They tied rope around their chests, securing them in place.

As they walked toward the door, she jerked her head toward them.

"Hey, assholes."

"Should we gag her too?" the first man asked.

Her eyes went wide and she shook her head.

"Then shut the fuck up. If I hear one word out of you, I'll come back in and gag you. We'll be outside."

After he'd slammed the door, Sierra tried to scoot her chair away from the table. It wouldn't budge, as if it had been bolted to the floor.

"Shit!"

"We are so fucked," Kyle said. "Mom's never going to find us here. Do you think they're going to kidnap her too?"

"I don't know." But she silently hoped they would, because at least then it would mean she wasn't dead.

17

Luke leapt out of bed and grabbed his SIG from the nightstand. He raced to the door and stood with his back to the wall. With the streetlights out, the entire house was cloaked in darkness. If he tried to use a flashlight, he might as well pin a bull's-eye on his forehead. He peeked into the hall, but couldn't make out a thing.

He'd left his pack in the living room so he wouldn't be able to get his night vision monocular without putting himself into the line of fire. He closed his eyes and listened for any hint of movement in the hall. As a SEAL, he'd been tasked with breaching enemy bases in the middle of the night, but there'd always been at least some ambient light.

After stalking halfway down the hall, he heard

another crunch of glass coming from the kitchen. He held his gun close to his chest. If someone tried to grab it, he'd have a better shot at retaining it if he kept it out of reach.

As he moved into the living room, he tried to pinpoint Boyd's location. He'd left him sitting near the back door. Was he still back there? Was he somewhere else in the house? He couldn't call out to him without risking his own life.

The door to the garage swung open.

Luke froze as someone stepped into the kitchen. More glass crackled when the intruder reached the sink.

Luke carefully lifted his foot straight up, toes pointing down to avoid snagging on the carpet. He placed the outside of his foot down first, pressing the ball of his foot into the floor and rolling from the outside in. After bringing his heel down, he slowly shifted his weight to that foot. He repeated the process with his other foot, making a soundless approach.

The faint outline of a man stood out against the midnight blue sky in the window. Less than two feet from the man, Luke raised his gun to the back of his head. He took a final step forward, pressing the barrel of the gun to the back of his head.

"Don't fucking move."

"Holy shit, don't shoot. It's me," Boyd said.

"What the fuck?" Luke stuffed his gun in his waistband. "What the hell are you doing? I almost shot you."

"Jesus, I didn't even hear you coming."

"I thought someone else was in the house. I heard glass breaking."

"The cat was meowing again. I was trying to find more food and I kicked a piece of glass."

"Did you cut yourself?"

"No. I kept my shoes on. I didn't hear anything, so I doubt anyone else is in the house," Boyd said.

"I'll check anyway."

Luke flicked on a flashlight. An unopened can of cat food sat on the counter. The cat was perched next to it. She let out a demanding meow.

"I'm working on it."

When Boyd grabbed a can opener, the cat trotted over to rub her face against his hand. Luke left them and headed back through the house to make sure they were alone.

After confirming no one else was in the house, he returned to find the cat face down in the bowl. She'd already scarfed half a can of food.

"I'm wide awake now," Luke said. "You should get some sleep. I'm guessing we only have an hour or so before sunrise. I'd like to get on the road at first light."

"Me too. I want to get home today. I don't need to sleep. I'm wide awake too."

"You need to be fully alert. Whoever tore through this neighborhood could still be out there. If you're too sleepy—"

"I found caffeine pills in one of the kids' dresser drawers," Boyd said.

"You searched the rooms again?"

"I was bored."

"You were supposed to be on guard."

"After I took those pills I was so alert I could hear my own heartbeat."

"Probably because it was trying to explode out of your chest."

"Nah, the ticker's just fine. Also, I'm too excited to try to sleep. If you were this close to home, you wouldn't sleep either."

"You're right," Luke said. Jealousy flashed through him for a moment. "Let's get you home."

"What about the cat?"

"We can't take her with us."

"Yeah, but we can't leave her here either," Boyd said.

As Luke scrubbed his hand over his face, he tried to come up with a good solution.

"We could leave all the cans of food open and leave as much water as possible."

A key scraped into the front door. Luke whipped around, gun drawn. Boyd grabbed the can opener and wielded it like a hammer.

The door opened and two kids ran into the house. One was a boy, about ten years old. The other, a girl, around seven. The moment the kids spotted them, they shrieked.

"Someone's in the house," one yelled.

A woman raced inside to grab them. She pushed them behind her.

"Who are you?" she demanded.

"We, uh…We were using your house as shelter."

"We fed the cat," Boyd said.

"Brutus!" the girl yelled. She raced out from behind her mom and headed for the cat.

"Madeline, get back here," her mom snapped.

"We don't mean any harm," Boyd said.

"Then why's he still pointing a gun at me?"

Luke lowered his arm, but didn't put the gun away.

"Is anyone else with you?" he asked.

"No. Why?" Fear flashed in her eyes. "Please don't hurt us. We walked all night to get home from my parents' house. We left to check on them two days ago."

"Where's your husband?" Luke asked.

"He died three years ago, cancer."

"I'm sorry for your loss. We're not going to hurt you. We were just leaving."

"We were trying to figure out what to do with your cat," Boyd said. When she gave him a horrified look, he quickly added, "We weren't going to hurt her. We were trying to figure out how to help her without taking her with us."

"Him," the boy whispered. He remained partially hidden behind his mother.

"Sorry," Luke said. "We've got to get on the road. We're trying to get back to our own families."

"We didn't ransack your house," Boyd said.

Luke groaned. He'd been hoping to get out before she realized everything was gone. If they tried to stop and help everyone along the way, they'd never make it home.

"What do you mean?" she asked.

"Before we got here, someone broke into your house and stole all of your food," Luke said.

"What?" She pushed past him, apparently more concerned about the lack of food than with the presence of a gun.

As she tore open cupboards, Luke jerked his head toward the front door. Boyd nodded and started slowly moving toward the living room. They had to get their packs before they could leave.

The woman burst out laughing.

"This is unbelievable," she said as tears rolled down her cheeks. "My parents begged me to stay with them and I told them we had more food at our house. There's nothing left. Nothing."

"I'm sorry," Luke said. "But it's good you weren't here when they got here. Your neighbors are dead."

"Dead?" The color faded from her face.

"We haven't checked all of the houses. Last night we were trying to find a place to stay. The neighbors between here and the main street are dead. We didn't kill them, we found them that way."

"I have to go back to my parents' house."

"It's your best option," Luke said.

"It's a ten-mile walk to get back."

"You could rest before you leave," Boyd said.

She shook her head and stared at the cat as if trying to decide what to do.

"Thank you for feeding him."

"We didn't kill your neighbors or break in."

"I know. You don't have any blood on you. Well, except on your pants. What happened to your leg?"

"Gunshot."

"What?" Her eyebrows jolted up.

"It happened yesterday. I'm okay though. It's only a graze."

"Let me see it." When he didn't move, she added, "I'm a nurse."

"Okay."

He sat in a kitchen chair and held the flashlight over the gash. Although it was still red, the streaks emanating from the wound had faded.

"Who stitched you up?" she asked.

"I did."

"It looks like Dr. Frankenstein got ahold of you."

"I thought the stitches were good."

"Serviceable, but you're going to have one hell of a scar."

"I'm not worried about that. I'm more worried about infection."

"I've got some antibiotics in my night stand."

"Uh, so about those…"

"You took them."

"Yes."

"So you did steal from me."

"Just the antibiotics. We didn't think you'd be back," Boyd said.

"I wasn't using them anymore," she said. "So go ahead. Take them."

"Aren't you supposed to take all of them until you run out?" Luke asked.

"Typically, yes. But that was my backup prescription."

"Why did you have a backup?"

"In case I ever needed them, but couldn't afford a doctor."

A ball of tightness formed in Luke's gut. He'd turned into the one thing he swore he'd never be: a thief. Although he didn't have any way of knowing what they were for, or when the homeowners would be back, he could have waited until they found a pharmacy. Guilt and shame rose up to claim him.

"I'm sorry I took your meds."

"You needed them. It's not the end of the world…well, maybe it is the end of the world, but you needed them. Don't worry about it. I'm sure my pill-popping mother has cases of pharmaceuticals at her house," she said with a wry smile.

"Thank you."

"Good luck out there," she said. "I can't tell you how many times I had to hide the kids. This place is overrun with gangs."

"They were armed and organized before the bombs. They're the worst threat out there."

"No. The worst threat's in here." She put her hand over her heart. "People are running out of food and water. They're starting to give up already. I see it in their eyes. At first everyone was furious, demanding to know how this could have happened. This is America, for crying out loud. But after almost two weeks, people are starting to realize how bad it's going to get.

Some people are ready to dig in and find a way to survive. Others have already resigned themselves to death. It's pathetic. People need to come together as a community."

"Are there people still left near your parents' house? *Good people*," he clarified.

"Yeah. They've lived in the same neighborhood for forty years. All of the neighbors know each other."

"Good. Then you have a chance. The only way to survive now is to work together."

"That's the plan. Take care."

Boyd walked back into the kitchen with his pack on his shoulders. He handed the other one to Luke. As they headed toward the door, Luke glanced back at the kids. Light still shone in their eyes. He hoped no one would snuff it out.

LUKE SAT on the edge of a freeway overpass as he popped another antibiotic pill into his mouth and washed it down with a swig of water. He peeled back the bandage on his leg. Even though he'd been walking all day, the redness and swelling had diminished significantly. He didn't have enough pills for a full course of treatment, but hopefully it would be enough to get him home. A little rest and tender loving care from Liz would go a long way toward making him feel better.

"How many miles do we have to go?"

"Only two more," Boyd said. "We're two exits from my street."

"So we should get there before sunset."

"Easily. I can't wait to see Vicki and the kids. You should spend the night. We'll have a big barbecue to celebrate."

"As much as I'd love to fall face-first down into a bed, I have to get home. I'll walk as far as I can tonight. If I don't make it all the way, I'll camp away from the road. Most of the land near the cabin is a protected wildlife sanctuary, so the human population is low. I doubt someone's going to put a bullet in my head in the middle of the night. But a mountain lion might decide to snack on me." He grinned.

"Not enough meat on your bones," Boyd said. "He'll have to chew you up to get at the bone marrow."

"Funny."

"I haven't felt this good in almost two weeks. Just knowing I'm this close to home is better than snorting an eightball off a hooker's ass."

"That's just—wow."

"I'm kidding. Come on, you grew up in the eighties."

"I was a teenager."

"Old enough for hookers and blow."

Luke side-eyed him.

"What can I say?" Boyd held his hands up and shrugged. "I was a wild child in Riverside."

"You don't seem like the type."

"My best friend died on my seventeenth birthday. He got some bad shit. I went cold turkey after that, turned my life around."

"Damn, that's terrible."

"Worst birthday present ever...or the best depending on how you look at it. In a way, he saved my life. I wouldn't be the man I am today if that hadn't happened."

"I guess that's one way of looking at it."

"I'm not gonna lie and tell you it was totally easy to quit. I had way too much time on my hands and no friends. I had to cut everyone from the scene out of my life."

"What did you do to stay busy?" Luke asked.

"Worked with an animal rescue organization."

"Really?"

"Yep. I could wrangle the meanest, growliest dogs in the county because I understood them. They'd been hurt in some way. They were distrustful and ready to lash out at anyone and everyone, so I'd wait them out. Show them I wasn't leaving until they came with me. I can't tell you how many I rescued, but I can tell you, they all had a hand in rescuing me from my demons. I met Vicki at the shelter."

"Really?"

"Yep. Her mom was the manager. Vicki would head over there after school and sit in the office doing homework. She's a couple of years younger than me."

"Liz is younger than me too. How'd you get her to go out with you? I figure her mom had to be watching her like a hawk."

"She was, but that made Vicki even more irresistible. Forbidden fruit. I did have to wait until she turned eighteen, but I asked her out the next day. Her mom wasn't too pleased at first, but I won her over. We got married a year later."

"You said you have three kids?"

"The first one was born nine months after we got married. Molly's twenty now. Dean came two years later, then Sam two years after that. He's sixteen now. Two more years and we're done raising kids."

"You never really finish raising them. My daughter Sierra is nineteen, but she's still a kid in a lot of ways. I worry about her. I think we sheltered her too much. I don't know if she's ready for the kind of world we're living in."

"This is going to be a sink or swim world. Without power, food, water, and jobs, everyone's going to have to either figure out how to live real quick, or die trying."

"The first year will be the worst. People are going to starve to death or get killed. After you get settled at home, you need to go out and get as many supplies as you can. Food, water, fuel for cooking, and a way to defend your home. If you start cooking barbecue and everyone else is starving, they're going to follow the smell and find you."

"I hadn't considered that." Boyd scratched at his beard.

"You'll have to be really careful. Set up some kind of perimeter defense, maybe put someone on watch. Do the kids still live with you? The older ones?"

"All three are still living at home. Molly wanted to take a gap year after high school. I was against it, but Vicki insisted on letting her bum around Europe. I gave in. Happy wife, happy life."

"I know what you mean." Luke smiled as he fished a bag of beef jerky from his pack. He bit into the salty toughness and sighed. Fortunately he'd be able to eat something else when he got back to the cabin. Anything else would do. "So what's Molly doing now? Does she work?"

"She set up a blog and has been doing YouTube makeup videos. I don't understand how it all works, but she's making some money from affiliate sales.

18

Elijah clenched his fists under his office desk as Turner relayed the events at the cabin. Although they'd captured the brats, they hadn't located the woman. Two of his men remained at the cabin waiting for her to arrive, while several others set out into the forest to look for her. So far, they hadn't brought her back.

"Your mission isn't complete," Elijah said.

"I know. My men will bring her back as soon as they find her," Turner said.

"Where are the kids?"

"In the Olmens' old house."

"Are they secure? I can't have them escaping."

"They aren't going anywhere. I have to tell you,

getting more manpower is making everything much easier to control," Turner said.

"We need even more men."

"How many are you thinking? Five? Ten?"

"Let's start with five more. We'll bring them on five at a time until we're fully operational. I want a group out hunting for supplies at all times. Another to protect the community. Another for extra projects. And of course, they'll all need to have time off, so we'll need multiple teams."

"Let me run some numbers and get back to you," Turner said. "We should be able to recruit enough men within a month."

"Good. I couldn't run this place without you," Elijah said.

Although he didn't want to share power with anyone else, he had to give Turner credit for everything he'd accomplished. As second in command, he'd proved to be a good soldier. Exactly the kind of man Elijah wanted by his side.

"I'm planning on leading a sweep of the forest," Turner said. "After that, I'll hike into town and look for more men."

"Good. I'm going to talk to the kids and see if I can get any more information."

"That girl has a mouth on her. If I were her dad, I'd wash it out with soap and tan her hide."

"I'll keep that in mind," Elijah said.

"I should be back by sundown."

After Turner left, Elijah unlocked the bottom drawer in his desk. He retrieved a bottle of whiskey and filled half a glass. He kicked it back, enjoying the way it burned down his throat. Although he didn't have the mother yet, he had her kids, so it was only a matter of time before he could get rid of them for good.

He used a trail behind the church to get to the Olmen house. Three guards stood sentry. They snapped to attention when he approached.

"Good morning, sir," Gunther said.

"Good morning. Are they still inside?"

"Yes. We nailed the windows and back door shut. The only way out is past us."

"Excellent. I'm going in to talk to them. You and your men can take a break. Go get yourself some breakfast. Come back in fifteen minutes," Elijah said.

"Yes, sir."

He waited until the men disappeared around a bend in the road before unlocking the front door. His pistol shifted in his waistband. Even though he wasn't going hungry, he'd lost enough weight in the last few weeks to loosen his pants. Once he got his teams in place, he'd have more access to food and he'd be able to bulk up.

Gloomy light filtered into the house through yellow curtains. The kids sat in chairs around the kitchen table. Sierra glared as he approached.

"Where's your mother?"

"Like we're going to tell you," the boy child said.

"What's your name, son?"

"Kyle, and I'm not your son."

"Kyle. It's very nice to finally meet you."

"Don't listen to a word he says," Sierra said. "He's a liar."

"Am I? What exactly have I lied about? You don't even know me."

Sierra pressed her lips together and shook her head. Defiant little bitch.

"Are you hungry?" Elijah asked. "Thirsty?"

"I could go for some water." Kyle flashed a silencing look at his sister. Maybe he was the weaker of the two, the easier one to break.

Elijah walked into the kitchen and pulled open several cabinets before finding a glass. He filled it with water from a pitcher on the counter. As far as he knew, the Olmens hadn't returned. Maybe the guards had left the water in view to torment the kids. Or they were using it for themselves.

"You can each have as much water as you can drink as soon as you tell me where your mother's hiding."

"Why do you want her?" Sierra asked.

"I want to talk to her."

"Why?"

"We need to have an adult conversation about a few things."

"Why do you keep bothering us?" she whined. "Why don't you leave us alone? We didn't do anything to you."

"Oh, but you did." He swung a chair around and straddled it. He took an exaggerated sip before setting the glass on the table. "Before you showed up, we were a peaceful community. Now, there's dissent. People are questioning my rules—our rules."

"How could Sierra make people question you?" Kyle asked. "I don't get it."

"There are women in my flock who think we should all be equal, but it's impossible. A group like ours needs strong leadership, and I'm their leader. They shouldn't be questioning me."

"Why not?" Sierra asked. "Why should anyone listen to you? Did they choose you as their leader, or did you just take over?"

"It's my church. I was appointed by God."

"I highly doubt He would appoint someone like you. You're an egotistical asshole out for himself. Adam told me about how you starved him and his mom for no reason."

"I had a reason."

"What reason?"

"That's none of your business."

"Was his mom one of the women who questioned you?" she asked. "That's my guess. I bet you didn't like it. You don't like strong women who can outthink you. Women like my mom."

"Silence!" Elijah slammed his fist against the table hard enough to knock the glass over. Water splashed across the table. The glass rolled toward the edge. He made no effort to stop it as it dropped to shatter on the floor. "You will tell me where she is, or I will make you regret it."

"How are you going to do that, Mr. Man of God?" she asked. "Are you going to starve us too? Torture us? My mom's going to come and get us and destroy you. Once your stupid flock finds out that you're kidnapping and starving people, they will run you out of the community. Men like you can only survive by keeping people in a state of fear. Once they know the truth, they'll see you're nothing but a charlatan. A false prophet. They talk about people like you in the Bible. You use religion to further your own agenda. There's nothing but greed and hate in your soul."

"You little bitch." Elijah stood so fast that the chair toppled over. "I could kill you right now. I could kill your brother and bury you both. No one would ever find you and your mother would spend the rest of her short, miserable life looking. I'd let her search and suffer until I got bored, then I'd kill her too."

Kyle's eyes welled with tears. At least Elijah was getting through to one of them.

"I don't want to do any of that," Elijah said as he moved closer to Kyle. "Just tell me where she is. Once I'm able to talk some sense into her, everything will be back to normal."

"She—"

"Shut up, Kyle!"

"He's going to kill us."

"If he wanted to kill us, he would have done it already. He needs us alive because he's using us as bait. Don't be so naïve," she snapped. "We're not telling you shit. So get the fuck out of here. I'm not afraid of you. Our mom will come. She will find us, and she will tear down your wall of bullshit."

Elijah strode over to slap her hard across the face. A red handprint marked one cheek. After a second blow to the other side, she had matching splotches. He walked into the kitchen and grabbed a knife from a block on the counter. The shiny steel blade glimmered in a shaft of light. Without hesitation, he returned to stab the knife into the kitchen table directly in front of Sierra.

"You have one hour to think about how much you value being alive. When I come back, you'd better tell me where she is, or I'll start cutting off fingers."

He jerked the knife out of the table and tossed it on the counter. Disgusted by the expression of utter contempt on the kids' faces, he took long steps toward the door. He slammed it behind him and sucked in a cooling breath of air. It had taken every ounce of self-control not to cut the little bitch's tongue out.

For now, he'd have to keep the little bastards alive. But as soon as he captured their mother, he was going to kill them all.

LIZ UNLOADED the last bags of food and added them to the pile around the campfire. The rising sun did little to dispel the chill in the air. Each day brought them closer to winter. Normally winters in southern California were mild. It wasn't unusual to hang out at the beach on Christmas. However, this year she doubted she'd be running around in a bikini.

"That's the last of it," she said. "Since we have the least food at my house because of the robbery, I'd like to take half back to my family. The other half can be split amongst the other households. Unless you'd like to start a community stockpile."

"You can't be serious," Irene said.

"Why not?" Liz snapped. Why was Irene always at her throat? The woman fought against everything she'd tried to accomplish, including this.

"Everyone but Sandy and Edwin sent a family member to help get food. They risked their lives, so the food should be split equally. I can't imagine that being up for debate," Irene said.

"I have to agree," Burt said. "Not only did I risk my life, but we used my truck. My gas. I could have lost the truck when that mob almost ambushed us."

"I understand where you're coming from," Liz said. "But you all have food stockpiles. I have nothing. We ate the last can of food yesterday. If I only take back a quarter of what we found, it's only going to last us a week. If that."

"We can go on another supply run when you're out," Harvey said.

"I don't know that I'm willing to risk the truck again," Burt said.

"What else were you planning on using it for?" Franklin asked. "We can't get much use out of it for anything other than supply runs."

"We?" Burt raised a brow. "It's *my* truck. It doesn't

belong to you. You're trying to start up some communist bullshit right now."

"It's not communist," Liz said. "It's neighbors helping neighbors."

"Look, we're all tired and need sleep," Harvey said. "For now, let's split it up equally. We can figure out next steps tomorrow. We'll have clearer heads after we've had time to rest."

As much as Liz wanted to stay and continue to argue, she couldn't wait to get back. After spending half the night on high alert, a soft, comfortable bed sounded like heaven.

"Okay," she said. "We'll split it equally."

As they worked to divide the food, she tried to sneak extra protein into her pile. Burt gave her the side-eye, so she stopped. Five bags of canned food and snack items. Five. She'd have to ration the hell out of it to make it last a week. Hopefully the kids would understand.

"I'll see you tonight," she said.

"Sundown at the fire pit. We can talk then," Harvey said.

She carried two bags in one hand and three in the other. The combined weight of all the food dragged her shoulders down. Although she wasn't a weak woman, the strain of being awake almost twenty-four hours was taking its toll.

The walk through the woods took twice as long as usual. She stopped several times to set the bags down to give her arms a rest. Maybe she'd underestimated the amount of food. Maybe it would last longer than a week. She wouldn't know until she sat down to do some meal planning. At least that would bring some semblance of normalcy back into her life.

Before the bombs, she'd planned all of the meals for the week on Sunday morning. She'd go to the store and get everything she needed and would cook the casseroles that night. It bought her extra time during the week. Although people probably thought she sat around eating bonbons and watching soap operas all day, a lot of work went into being a mom. Cleaning the house took an entire day. Then there was laundry, dishes, shuttling Kyle to soccer practice. It all took time. If things ever got back to normal, she'd welcome the hectic schedule.

As she approached the cabin, birds chirped in the trees. The scene was worthy of a painting. The cabin's peaceful serenity had called to her soul when they'd first seen it. It had been the best purchase they'd ever made.

When she reached the door, she knocked three times. No one moved inside. Sierra would be on patrol right now, but Kyle should be home. Unless he was sleeping in again.

She knocked again.

Nothing.

Well, Kyle could sleep like the dead.

She picked up the bags and headed toward the back door. The window closest to his bed on the second floor looked over the back porch. She might have to lob a rock up there to wake him up.

As she rounded the corner adrenaline ripped through her belly, leaving a searing line of pain in its wake. Ripped from its hinges, the back door lay on the floor. She dropped the bags and ran inside. Absolute destruction covered the living room. Lamps had been knocked over. All of the guns were missing.

"Kyle!"

"Sierra!"

She scrambled up the steps to the loft. Empty.

Downstairs, she checked the bathroom and all of the cabinets to make sure they weren't hiding from whoever had destroyed the house.

She didn't find a single trace of them. Kyle had been taken. She'd spent too much time hunting for food and had left them vulnerable to attack. How could she have been so stupid? She should have taken them with her.

She had to find Sierra. Today she was scheduled to be on the highest peak on patrol from sunrise to noon. She had to be there.

As she rushed up the hill toward the peak, her heart thundered. Please let her be there. Please.

When she reached the lookout location, she dropped to her knees. Owen, Burt's son, turned to stare at her.

"What's going on?" he asked.

"Where's Sierra?"

"I'd love to know. She was supposed to be up here to relieve me an hour ago. She never showed up."

"Did you see anyone near the house?" she asked. "Someone broke in. I think they kidnapped the kids."

"Oh crap." His gaze dropped to his feet.

"What?"

"I kinda fell asleep last night."

"What? When?"

"Right before sunrise. It's boring as hell sitting up here all night. Nothing ever happens. It's stupid. I don't even know why we have patrols."

She literally wanted to strangle him with her bare hands.

"You idiot! You were supposed to keep watch. You let them take my kids."

"I was tired."

She turned on her heel and ran down the hill toward Harvey's house. When she spotted him in the backyard feeding the goats, she waved frantically.

"They took—" She gasped for air. "They took the kids."

"What? Who took what kids?"

"My kids." She skidded to a stop just outside the gate. "The preacher's men. They came. They took the kids."

"Are you sure they're not out on patrol? Isn't Sierra supposed to be on the hill right now?"

"Yes! The cabin was tossed. The guns are gone. The kids. Oh my God." She tried to calm her racing heart but couldn't catch a deep breath.

"Let's round up the group," Harvey said. "Go get Burt, I'll get Franklin and Edwin."

"Okay."

She ran the entire way to Burt's house. When she arrived, his wife Tawney was sitting in a chair on the front porch. She jumped up.

"Is everything okay?" Tawney asked.

"No. I need… Where's Burt?

"Sleeping."

"They took my kids."

"The preacher?"

"Yes."

"Good God." Tawney brought her hand to her mouth. "I'll get him."

While Liz waited, she struggled to catch her breath. Were the kids still alive? What did he want with them? Why was he coming after her family again? Why was any of this happening?

Burt raced outside, still pulling on his belt as he stumbled onto the porch.

"We're meeting at the fire pit."

Everyone from the community reached the fire pit at the same time.

"We need a plan to get them back," Harvey said.

"You'd be risking your life," Irene said.

"Shut up, woman," he snapped. "Liz is a part of our community and so are her kids. I've about had it with your damn mouth. Now, we're going to get her kids back and end this bullshit with the preacher once and for all. If you're not going to take part, then go home. I don't have time to deal with any crap. We don't know what he's doing to them right now, so we need to move."

"What's the plan?" Burt asked.

"We need to find them first," Liz said. "We can't make a plan unless we know for sure where they are and what we're up against."

"Okay. We'll go in teams of two. Everyone have a gun?" Harvey asked.

Everyone nodded and paired up. Liz stepped closer to Harvey while Irene stood on the sidelines, glaring.

"We move out now," Harvey said. "We can't go

running over there, guns blazing. Keep a low profile. We gather information, then we take action. Got it?"

When everyone agreed, he headed into the forest. Liz walked shoulder to shoulder with him. For the first time since the bombs dropped, someone actually gave a shit about her and the kids. In fact, everyone but Irene joined the reconnaissance mission. Well screw her. She could go fuck herself for all Liz cared.

As she trekked across the stream, Liz steeled her spine. She'd get her kids back no matter what it took, even if it meant dying for them. Rage burned through her veins. The preacher didn't know what he'd done. He'd provoked a mother's vengeance, and she'd rain fire and brimstone down on his soul the likes of which the world had never seen.

19

Luke hung back as Boyd pulled a key from his pocket. As he scanned the neighborhood, Luke caught a flash of movement three houses down. There, by the bushes. He narrowed his gaze and squinted against the setting sun. Shadows shifted, but he couldn't make out any particular form. Maybe it had been a trick of the light.

After unlocking the door, Boyd stepped to the side. They'd already agreed to go in slow, Luke first, Boyd as backup.

Luke pushed the door. He stood to one side and scanned for people as the door creaked open. The entryway was clear, so he took a step inside. A narrow hallway led to the living room and the kitchen. Boyd had drawn a map of the layout so Luke wouldn't go in completely blind.

As Luke peeked around the corner into the living room, his heart stopped. Blood spatter arced across the wall behind the couch. A naked woman lay slumped over, her throat slit.

An inhuman scream erupted from Boyd. He shoved Luke out of the way and threw himself at the woman's feet. He lifted her chin. Vacant eyes stared at nothing. He howled like a dying wolf. Before Luke could react, Boyd jumped up and ran down the hall toward the bedrooms.

"Wait!" Luke yelled. They hadn't cleared the rest of the house.

"NOoooo!"

"Shit."

Luke quickly checked the kitchen before jogging down the hall. In the first room, he spotted a teenage boy. Dead from a gunshot wound to the forehead. In the second bedroom, another boy, slightly older, lay facedown in a pool of caked blood. But the true horror lay in the third.

He walked in to find Boyd frantically pulling the rope which bound his daughter spread eagle to the bed. Luke shoved his gun in his waistband and pulled a knife from his pack. He quickly helped untie her.

Boyd pulled her into his arms while struggling to

pull a blanket over her exposed body. Tears streamed down his face.

"She's dead," he moaned.

As he sobbed, Luke double-checked the rest of the house to make sure they were alone. He returned to find Boyd rocking his daughter. Rigor mortis had come and gone, leaving her limp. One of her legs slid off the edge of the bed. Boyd carefully pulled it back onto the bed.

"I never should have gone to Vegas. I never should have left them alone."

"There's no way you could have known this would happen," Luke said.

"I was off having fun while they were being tortured."

"No. This didn't happen until after the bombs dropped. You were already headed home by then."

"It doesn't matter when it happened," Boyd snapped. "I wasn't here. I *failed* them."

Luke pressed his lips together. Trying to reason with him right now was pointless. He was too consumed by grief to listen to reason. Luke couldn't imagine the pain of losing his entire family. Nothing he could say would help ease Boyd's suffering, so he kept his mouth shut. He slowly backed out of the room and headed back to the front door.

As he reached to close it, he hesitated. He took a

step out onto the porch and studied the neighborhood. A glint of light flashed from a house across the street, several doors down. He eased back inside and closed the door. As he pushed the curtain aside, the flash disappeared. He stayed still, waiting for another glimpse.

After several minutes, he gave up. It was probably nothing anyway.

He headed back into the bedroom where Boyd cradled his daughter. In the span of only a few minutes, he looked as if he'd aged twenty years. His typically exuberant smile had been replaced by a scowl.

"Who could have done this?" he muttered.

"I don't know. We might never know."

"There has to be a clue. Something."

"It was probably a gang." As soon as the words left his mouth, he regretted them. Boyd shook his head from side to side while mumbling under his breath.

"No. Not a gang. No graffiti. They would have left some kind of sign."

"We might never know."

"We? How the fuck is this about you?" Boyd eased his daughter to one side and slipped off the bed. He stalked toward Luke and scowled. "This isn't about you."

"I didn't mean it like that."

Boyd jabbed a finger into Luke's chest. "How the fuck did you mean it?"

"I—"

"You slowed me down. I could have been here faster if it weren't for you."

"What? I was the one who wanted to keep moving. You were perfectly happy to spend hours looking for food and water."

"I needed fuel."

"*We* needed fuel. Whether or not you want to admit it, it took teamwork to get here. Neither of us would have made it alone."

Boyd growled and rushed forward, tackling Luke to the ground. Luke shoved at his bulk and tried to pry him off. A fist smashed into his face. His lip split, the metallic taste of blood spread across his tongue. Before he could react, Boyd slammed his other fist into his face. Luke reached up and jabbed him in the eye. Boyd roared and jerked back. Luke rolled to his knees and shoved Boyd.

Instead of falling backward, Boyd grabbed Luke's shoulders. Luke locked his hands on Boyd's and head-butted him. As Boyd tumbled back, Luke jumped to his feet.

"Stop trying to fight me. You won't win."

Boyd snarled as he used the edge of the bed as

leverage to stand. He wiped a bloody hand across the back of his mouth. A thin trail of blood seeped from one corner of his mouth.

"You're pissed, I get it. But don't think for a second that you get to take it out on me."

"Go fuck yourself," Boyd snapped.

"You need to calm the fuck down."

"Do I? Really?" Boyd glared.

"You know what, I don't need this shit. Have a nice life." Luke turned and stalked toward the front door.

"Good luck, asshole."

"Dick," Luke grumbled. Part of him understood Boyd's need to lash out, but he wasn't going to stick around and be his punching bag. He adjusted his pack as he walked down the hall. Anger tightened his chest. It was all he could do to keep himself from going back to pound Boyd into the ground.

As he reached for the front doorknob, Boyd yelled.

"Wait! Wait!" He ran down the hall. "Look what I found!"

Boyd uncurled his fingers to reveal an old class ring.

"Congratulations," Luke said dryly.

"You don't understand. I know who did this. I know who killed my family.

"What do you mean you know who killed your family?" Luke asked.

"Those bastard Nicklinsons. I saw the way they looked at my wife and daughter, but they never did anything. They never said anything. I had no idea. No idea. I should have known. I never should have left them alone."

"How do you know it was them?"

"This." Boyd held up the ring. "I caught Bart Nicklinson hanging around the sidewalk outside the house. I asked him if he needed something. He said he was out jogging and lost his ring. But it was sitting on his damn finger. When I pointed it out he laughed and said he didn't mean that ring. That one was his high school ring. It had his graduation year engraved on the side. From 1990. It's the same ring."

"Wait, back up. Who's Bart Nicklinson?"

"The son of a bitch who lives across the street."

"A few doors down on the right?"

"Yeah. Why? Did you see him?" Boyd stomped toward the door.

"No. Stop. Don't open the door. If it really was Nicklinson, he's probably watching the house. Earlier, I thought I saw a flash of light across the street about three houses down on the right."

"That's it. That's his house."

"Okay wait. You can't go running over there half-cocked."

"The hell I can't."

When Boyd tried to grab the doorknob, Luke gripped the back of his shirt and slammed him up against the wall.

"Calm the fuck down for two seconds. Shit."

"How calm would you be if the man who murdered your whole family was right across the street?"

"I'd be fucking pissed."

"Exactly." Boyd tried to move away from the wall, Luke pushed him back with his forearm.

"Wait. Hear me out. First of all, you don't know for sure it was him. It could be anyone's."

"No. See this?" He tilted the ring on its side. "Maryborn High. He told me it's on the East Coast. So there's no way it could belong to someone else."

"Even if it's his, it doesn't prove anything. He could have come in here before or after they were killed. He could have come to check on you guys to see how you were doing."

"No, he's not that kind of guy. He didn't give a shit about the neighborhood. He never went to any of the barbecues. Kept to himself."

Boyd stared off into space. The look in his eye curdled Luke's blood. He radiated pure rage. His knuckles were white; his fists, clenched. Murderous intent contorted his features. He was a powder keg of revenge, just waiting to explode.

"I'll make them suffer," Boyd whispered. He slowly turned his faced toward Luke. "If you're not going to help me, then get the fuck out of my house."

"Shit."

Luke ran his hand through his hair. How could he convince Boyd not to go over there and get himself killed? And why did he even care? Boyd had just cold-cocked him. He should let him go get his ass kicked, but he couldn't. If this Nicklinson guy really did kill Boyd's family, he wanted him to get justice.

"Look, I'll help you," Luke said. "But we can't go running over there without a plan."

"Dammit." Boyd spun around and punched a hole through the drywall.

"What the fuck?" Luke backed up a step.

"You're right, but I want to fucking kill him. Right now."

"I know. I know. But hear me out." He waited until Boyd made eye contact. "I think we should wait. It's almost sundown. We can afford to wait a few hours. Then we go on recon, stake the place out. Is anyone else living with him?"

"Porky, his son."

"Porky?"

"I don't know his real name. The little prick sits around watching TV all day. I see him in his living room sitting on his ass all the time." Boyd scratched the side of his face. "I wasn't spying. They always had the curtains open so I'd see him when I was out walking with the kids."

"Are they open right now?"

"Lemme check." Boyd pushed the curtain aside and looked outside. "No. They're closed."

"Okay, so we can't walk by and look inside."

"No, we're going to have to get into the house."

"Or, we could try drawing them out."

"How?"

"Create some kind of diversion. Start a fire."

"Then what?" Boyd asked.

"Then we hold them at gunpoint and get confirmation that they're the ones who did this."

"I know it was them. Both of them. There's no way one could take on four people."

"One of them could have used someone in your family as a hostage. Everyone else would have been forced to cooperate."

"Bart's not smart enough to pull something like that off alone. He had help."

"We can question them. Find out who was in on it."

"You think they're going to tell us?" Boyd laughed sharply. "Those lying bastards will deny everything."

"Maybe. But we have to try. Don't you want to know for sure? What if it wasn't them? If we kill them and they didn't do it, then we'd be murdering them."

"Fuck."

"Let's wait a couple of hours until it's dark."

"I can't just sit around."

"We won't." Luke swallowed and hoped he wasn't making a big mistake. "We'll be burying your family."

Boyd moaned and brought his hands up to cover his face. He walked into the living room, stumbled over the edge of the coffee table and plopped down next to his wife.

As he cried, Luke headed into the kitchen. He opened the fridge. The stench of rotting food mingled with the scent of death. He grabbed an unopened water bottle and slammed the door. The smell made him gag as he walked back into the living room.

"Here." He handed the bottle to Boyd who shook his head. "You need to drink."

"How can I go on without them?"

"You have to."

Boyd took the bottle and twisted off the cap. His red rimmed eyes shimmered with fresh tears.

"They were my life."

"I know."

"This is just...How do you bury your family?"

"We don't have to do it right now."

"No. I want to. They deserve to rest in peace. The shovels are in the garage."

After Luke retrieved the shovels, he leaned them against the wall outside on the back porch. He brushed his hands against his pants and slid open the door. Boyd hadn't moved from the couch, a forlorn expression on his face.

Instead of bothering him, Luke grabbed a shovel and headed into the backyard. A flowerbed formed a perimeter around the edge of the fence. Several tall shade trees blocked the setting sun. The rest of the space was covered in grass.

He picked a location near the back of the lawn and jabbed the shovel into the earth. With his boot, he pressed the edge down several inches before pulling up the first clump of dirt. He continued the process, ignoring the ache in his arms, occasionally stopping to wipe sweat from his eyes.

Halfway through the first grave, Boyd joined him outside. He didn't say a word as he picked up the other shovel and began digging the second grave. As they worked, several doves perched high up in the trees. Their lamenting whinny seemed appropriate. Maybe they'd been sent from Heaven to guide the souls of the dead.

It took three hours to finish the first two graves. After wrapping his wife in a sheet, Boyd carried her to the grave. Luke helped him lay her in her final resting place.

"I feel like I should say something," Boyd muttered.

Luke bowed his head.

"Vicki, baby I love you so much. I'm going to get justice for you. I swear it. I know you're not here anymore. You're up there looking down on me. Well, close your eyes, because you might not want to see what I'm about to do to the man who hurt you."

With that, Boyd shoveled a pile of dirt into the grave. He sobbed as he laid more dirt over his beloved wife.

His daughter followed. Then three hours later, his sons. By the time they'd buried Boyd's entire family, Luke arms burned and exhaustion sank into his bones. He dumped one last shovelful of dirt before tossing the shovel aside. He left Boyd at the graves. If it was him, he'd have wanted a moment alone.

Inside the house, Luke sat in a kitchen chair. He covered his face with his hands and tried to blot out the image of his family in a grave. He wasn't one to pray too often, but from the depths of his soul, he called out to God, silently asking him to please keep his family safe until he could return to protect them.

20

Liz hit the button on the walkie-talkie and whispered into it to give her location. She and Harvey lay on their bellies on a ridge overlooking the preacher's compound. Using a pair of binoculars, she scanned the dining area. Several men and women lingered at the picnic tables, while others filtered off toward other areas in the compound. Breakfast had ended thirty minutes earlier and she still hadn't spotted the preacher or her kids.

"We should move to another location," Liz said.

"Isn't this their main meeting place?"

"Yes. Everyone has to pass through here to get to the other areas. I thought we'd see them here."

"Maybe the kids aren't at the church. Maybe they're in one of the other houses," Harvey said.

"Could be," she said. "But I have a feeling the preacher's keeping the kids close. When we find him, we'll find them. Right now we can't see anything from this location. We should move."

"We can't risk being spotted. If they know we're spying on them, they'll bring in the rest of their patrol. As it is, they outnumber us two to one. Making the odds worse isn't going to help us at all."

Liz raised the binoculars and scanned the area. As much as she hated to admit it, he was right. She fought against the instinct to rush down and start shooting until someone told her where the kids were being held. Someone had to know. The preacher couldn't have kidnapped them without help.

She spotted movement out of the corner of her eye. As she lowered the binoculars, Melinda, Adam's mom, walked into the forest a hundred yards to her left. She was on her feet before Harvey could protest.

"Adam!" Melinda called. "Are you up here?"

"If you scream, I'll shoot." Liz stepped out from behind a tree and pointed her gun at the other woman.

"Liz?" Melinda slowly raised her hands in surrender. "Have you seen Adam? He's been missing since this morning. I got up and he was gone."

"Have you seen my kids?"

"Your kids? No. I haven't left the compound."

"I know the preacher has them. Where are they?" Liz's gun hand trembled.

"What do you mean he has them?"

"He kidnapped them last night. Or early this morning. I don't know. I wasn't there."

"Are you sure they're gone?"

"Yes. And he took them. I want my fucking kids back, Melinda. Where are they?"

"I think she's telling the truth," Harvey said. "She doesn't know."

"The hell she doesn't. She's one of them," Liz said.

"I don't know where your kids are. I don't even know where my son is," Melinda said. "I'm afraid…"

"What?" Liz lowered the gun but held it at her side.

"I'm afraid Elijah did something to Adam."

"Why?"

"He's missing and… I shouldn't have done it…"

"What did you do?"

"I challenged Elijah in front of everyone. This place is turning into a cult. He's been ruling over it like it's his own personal commune. I kept ignoring all the red flags. We have nowhere else to go. We could go home, but there's nothing there. We wouldn't have any food, any water, or any protection. But I'm done. As soon as I find Adam, we're leaving.

It's not safe here anymore, especially if he's kidnapping people."

"Adam could be with Sierra and Kyle," Liz said. "When you were at breakfast, did you hear or see anything unusual?"

Melinda frowned. Her gaze focused on a point in the distance before returning to Liz.

"I overheard Turner tell someone to bring food to the Olmens' house. But that's weird because the Olmens left over a week ago. As far as I know, no one is living there."

"Where is it?" Harvey asked.

"About a half mile up the road."

"We'll check it out," Liz said.

"Wait!" Melinda grabbed her arm. "You can't go running down there with guns. If the kids are there, you could shoot them by accident. If there are guards inside, they could shoot the kids."

"They might not even be in the house," Harvey said. "We need to do recon to find out."

"What if I did it for you?" Melinda said.

"Why would you help us?" Liz asked.

"Because I need to find Adam. Today's the last day I'm going to let Elijah control us. As soon as I get Adam, we're going home. We might end up starving to death, but at least we'd have a chance. We're not safe here. Three people have gone missing in the last week. Elijah keeps telling us that they chose to go home, but each of the missing people had fought with Elijah a few hours before they went missing. I think he killed them."

Liz's knees went weak. She wobbled toward the closest tree and leaned against it. What if he'd already killed her kids?

"They're probably still alive," Harvey said. "My guess is that he's using them as bait. Pull it together."

Liz took a breath and pushed off the tree.

"Let me go check the house," Melinda said. "I can get closer than you. I'll just tell them I'm looking for Adam. It's the perfect cover."

"How do we know we can trust you?" Liz asked. "How do I know you're not going to find Elijah and tell him we're up here?"

"Look at me." Melinda raised her arms to display a much-too-large tattered shirt. "Look at what he's doing to us. We're all hungry. Tired. Overworked. He sits there like a king, demanding we wait on him like slaves. I'm done. I don't care if you believe me or not, but I'm going to find my son."

"If he's at the house and you manage to get him out, will you at least come back to tell us if Sierra and Kyle are inside too?" Liz asked.

"You have my word, mother to mother."

Liz nodded. When Melinda turned to walk along

the tree line, Liz followed.

"You can't come with me," Melinda whispered over her shoulder. "They'll see you."

"I want to know the house's location."

"Okay. I'll take you as far as I can. But if they see us, we're all dead."

"They won't see us," Harvey said. "If you do find Adam, be careful. We don't know what the preacher's motive is for taking him. He could want you dead too. It sounds like he's weeding out troublemakers."

"I'll be careful."

As Liz picked a silent path through the forest, she studied Melinda's hunched shoulders. No one could fake such a defeated tone in their voice. Her heart went out to the other mother. Regardless of how they ended up with the preacher, they wanted out. And if Melinda helped her find Sierra and Kyle, Liz would do everything in her power to help her in return.

A few minutes later, Melinda stopped. She pointed at a house which was set back from the main road. Three men sat outside. They each had a rifle strapped to their chest.

"That's the Olmen house," Melinda whispered.

"They're guarding someone," Liz said. "What's your plan to find out who's inside?"

"I'm going to offer them food. I'm in charge of all the baking, so I can bring them cookies."

"You should have brought some with you," Liz said.

"I thought I'd find Adam in the forest. There wasn't any reason to bring cookies."

"Be careful," Liz said. "You don't know what their orders are. Maybe they're supposed to take you too."

Melinda's eyes went wide. Her head whipped toward the house, then back. "What if they make me go inside?"

"We'll find a way to rescue you," Liz said. "I highly doubt they have houses full of prisoners. Just be careful about the way you word things. Don't let on that you're looking for anyone but your son."

"I won't. I may not be the best liar ever, but they don't look very smart."

"Never underestimate the enemy," Harvey said.

"Okay."

As Melinda walked through the trees toward the house, Liz raised her rifle. She sighted one of the guards. Her finger shifted toward the trigger, but she paused. She couldn't kill them until she knew who was inside. If they'd help capture her kids, she'd shoot all three of them. But until she got confirmation of her kid's location, she couldn't make a move.

Liz frowned as Melinda's conversation with the guards continued. After ten minutes, she was ready to race down and wipe the smirks off the guards' faces, preferably with a few well-placed bullets. If Melinda didn't get her ass back up the hill soon, Liz was going down there.

"Patience," Harvey murmured.

"How patient would you be if your kids were missing?" she asked in a hushed tone.

"She'll be back soon. If we make hasty decisions, they could end up dead."

"I know." She swatted a fly away from her arm. "I just wish she'd hurry up."

"They're opening the door."

Liz grabbed the binoculars from him. The door cracked open to reveal a sliver of darkness. She couldn't see anyone, or anything for that matter. The guard slammed the door and pushed Melinda back. She screamed at him and pointed toward the church. The guard shook his head and smiled. When she reached to slap his face, he grabbed her wrist and twisted it behind her back. He whispered something that made her sag against the wall. The second he released her, she turned and ran down the road.

"She's escaping."

Liz jumped to her feet and raced along the tree line. Without knowing Melinda's motivation to run, Liz couldn't risk confronting her on the road. She kept pace with Melinda until she abruptly changed course and ran up the hill into the forest.

"They have them." Melinda bent over to catch her breath. "They have all of the kids."

"Did you see them? Are they alive?"

"Yes. And yes. They're alive."

"Why didn't they take you too?" Liz asked.

"I don't know."

"Maybe they have Adam for another reason," Harvey said. "Are you sure he's a prisoner?"

"He was tied to a chair," Melinda snapped. "Of course he's a prisoner. We have to rescue them. There're three of us and three guards. We can take them. You have guns."

"If we shoot them, everyone else will come running," Harvey said. "We don't know where the rest of their men are hiding. They could be staked out in the area. It's too risky to go down there right now."

"What are we going to do?" Melinda asked. "We can't leave them there."

"We're not going to leave them," Liz said. "We have more people who can help, but we need to get word to them. We need reinforcements."

"Where are they?"

"They're in a perimeter around the compound," Harvey said. "I'll radio our location and get them over here."

As Harvey stepped farther into the forest, Liz

took a step toward Melinda. She couldn't let her fall apart.

"We're going to get the kids back and we're going to make that bastard pay," Liz said. "You can cry all you want later, but right now, you need to help me come up with a plan. You know the routine better than any of us. If you were going to plan a rescue, what would you do? How would you do it? And when would you do it?"

Melinda sniffed a few times and wiped dampness from her eyes. After pulling herself together, she drew her shoulders back and returned to her full height.

"I'd do it at midnight. The guards do a shift change around that time. Adam used to go on patrol with the other men. He'd come home or leave at midnight depending on his shift."

"When's the other shift change?" Liz asked.

"Noon."

"Midnight it is."

Burt and Tawney reached the group first, followed by Franklin and Jamie. After introducing everyone, Liz explained the situation.

"How many men are on patrol at night?" Franklin asked.

"Five or six," Melinda said.

"Minus the three at the house," Liz said.

"No. Those guys are new. I've never seen them

before. And there could be more. Turner was gone for a few days. I saw him come back with five guys last night. Three of them are at the house," Melinda said.

"So he's bringing on new recruits," Harvey said.

"Sounds like it," Franklin said. "We need to distract the guards. A firefight is the last thing we want. We've got seven people. They could have ten. And we don't know anything about their locations."

"Maybe we should just do reconnaissance tonight," Burt said. "Wait until tomorrow night to make a move. The more information we can get, the better."

"We can't risk it," Liz said. "If we wait another night, the kids could be dead."

"My son's in there too. I don't want to wait. It has to be tonight."

"Okay," Harvey said. "We need to pull all of the guards away. How?"

"A fire," Burt said. "Are there any other abandoned houses?"

"Two. One's up by the church. They're using it to store firewood," Melinda said.

"That's perfect. It will burn for a long time," Liz said. "There's no running water, so it'll be hard to put out. We need to stay away from the stream. That's the first place they'll head."

"We have a few 55 gallon drums," Melinda said.

"How many?"

"Three."

"Not nearly enough," Liz said. "The fire will keep everyone occupied. No one will want it to spread. Who'll set the fire?"

"I'll do it," Burt said.

"He's always been a bit of a pyro," his wife said.

"The rest of you will provide cover fire if we end up in a gunfight. We'll probably have to break down the door or go in through a window," Liz said.

"I'd try a window. Easier to break," Harvey said.

"I saw a big one on the side of the house. We'll use that one," Melinda said.

"Good. We only have one shot at saving our kids. If we screw this up…"

"We won't," Harvey said. "As long as everyone does their part, we'll have your kids back tonight."

After agreeing to meet at the same location an hour before midnight, everyone but Liz and Melinda went home to try to get a few hours of sleep.

"I won't be able to sleep," Liz said.

"Me neither."

"We should at least go back to my house so I can get you a gun."

"I don't know how to shoot one," Melinda said.

"I'll show you. We can dry fire to pass the time."

"Dry fire?"

"No bullets. It's not the best way to train, but since we're pressed for time..."

"I really don't want to shoot anyone," Melinda said. "I'm not a violent person."

"How did you end up in the preacher's group?" Liz stepped over a fallen log as they headed back toward her cabin.

"I've been a part of that church for twenty years. The old pastor, God rest his soul, was the kindest, most gentle man I've ever known. I wept when he passed away. Elijah rose through the ranks and took over as the new pastor. I never did like him very much, but everyone embraced him, so I thought it was God's will. I can't understand how God could let such an evil man take over. How does that happen?"

"God doesn't have time to manage the day-to-day operations of every church on earth." Liz smiled. "But don't worry. When his time comes, he'll have some answering to do."

"I hope so. He's shaken my faith. I don't know what to believe anymore."

"Once you're free of that place, you'll feel much better."

"I hope you don't take this the wrong way, but in a strange way, I'm glad he took your kids too." Tears sprang into Melinda's eyes. "Without you and your friends, I'd never be able to rescue my son."

"You're stronger than you think," Liz said. "You're a survivor."

"Thank you."

"Where will you go after you get your son back?"

"Home, I guess. I don't know what's waiting there, but I don't have any place else."

"There are still good people left in the world. Maybe you'll find another community. God knows you can throw a rock in Orange County and hit a church."

"Isn't that the truth?" Melinda laughed.

As the hours ticked by, Liz listened to her recount stories about her family. The more she got to know Melinda, the more she liked her. She was a good woman trapped in a bad situation. Hopefully she'd find a way to make it in this world.

From now on only the strong would survive. The weak would be exploited and killed by people who grew more and more desperate as resources ran out. Was Luke okay? Was he still battling his way through the valley? Or had his luck run out?

She shook her head to clear it. Worrying about Luke wouldn't do a damn thing to help the kids. Luke wasn't here, but she was, and she would do whatever it took to get her kids back, even if it meant facing a hail of bullets and bloodshed.

21

Luke frowned as he leaned across the kitchen table to study the floorplan of the Nicklinson's house. The layout was similar to Boyd's place, but there were more blind corners and closets for people to hide in. He held a penlight over the top part of the map. With his finger, he drew a line in from one of the rear windows.

"We have to assume the doors are locked. If we try to breach through one of them, we might run right into a guard."

"You think they'll be posted at the doors?" Boyd asked. He stood shoulder to shoulder with Luke.

"Maybe. We don't know how many people are inside."

"It's just the two of them, Bart and Porky. The

wife left five years ago, haven't seen her since. We used to joke that he'd killed her and buried her in the backyard. Now I wonder if he did."

"You never really know your neighbors, do you?"

"Not really. But then again, do you really know anyone? People only show you one side of themselves. I don't know about you, but I try to keep my crazy in check. If anyone really knew what was going on in my head, they'd lock me up faster than the nuclear codes."

"Apparently they weren't locked up well enough."

"Not when you have crazy politicians in charge of them."

"I wonder if we hit back," Luke said.

"Hit who, the Chinese?"

"Whoever bombed us."

"I hope we find out one day. The lack of information is killing me," Boyd said.

"I hear you."

"So you're thinking the back window? Keep in mind, I only walked through that house once, years ago when the previous owners had an open house."

"Why'd you go to an open house in your own neighborhood?"

"Curiosity. Don't you ever wonder what the inside of other people's houses look like?"

"Not really," Luke said. "Although, my wife loves

going to the new home models. They've been building so many in Orange County that we turned it into a fun free thing to do on the weekends."

"Do you go every weekend?"

"Not every weekend. That would drive me nuts. But we go often enough. I don't mind indulging her fantasies. If she starts to really get excited about buying one of those huge houses, I remind her that someone's going to have to clean it, and it's not going to be me."

"Is that enough of a deterrent?"

"Sometimes. Usually she starts in on how we should hire a housekeeper. But who has enough money for that?"

"Rich people."

"Well, we're not rich. Not hurting for money, but not rich."

"After we get inside, which way should we head first?" Boyd asked.

"The back of the house. Clear that, then we work our way forward."

"I can't wait to put a bullet in that asshole's face."

"The temptation will be there, but until we know what we're dealing with, you have to try to stay calm."

Boyd grabbed a bottle of whiskey off of the table and took another swig.

"You should lay off that," Luke said. "You need to be alert. Ready for anything."

"I couldn't be more alert if you smashed a pair of cymbals against my ears."

"If you die, all of this will be for nothing."

"We're not dying today," Boyd said. "They are."

"Maybe."

"I know they did it. I'm going to make them pay."

Trying to argue with Boyd was pointless. Luke checked the magazine before jamming it back into his SIG. They only had one gun. Boyd had torn apart the house searching for his revolver, but had come up empty. It had been stolen too.

"Keep your flashlight off. There's a half moon up tonight. We'll use that light to navigate. I also have my night vision monocular in case we need it. I don't want to use it unless it's pitch black. Metal might reflect the moonlight and give away our approach."

He pulled the Bestguarder 6x50mm HD Digital Night Vision Monocular from his pack and shoved it into his front pocket.

"I'm ready." Boyd grabbed the tire iron he'd retrieved from the garage.

"Stay smart. Stay safe."

"Whatever it takes to get justice."

Luke switched off the penlight and tucked it into

his waistband. Worst case scenario, he wanted access to light fast. Although he wanted to trust Boyd, he couldn't. The calm exterior he'd displayed over the last hour crumbled every time he talked about revenge. As long as he didn't go off half-cocked, they'd have a shot at finding out the truth about Boyd's family.

Outside, chilly air whipped through his hair. A bead of sweat snaked down his spine. He'd been awake almost twenty-four hours without a break. Boyd had been awake over thirty-six hours.

Luke squatted low as he ran across the street. When he reached the fence to the target's backyard, he grabbed it and vaulted over. He unlocked the gate from the other side and let Boyd in. He closed the gate behind Boyd, but didn't lock it in case they needed to make a fast escape. They'd run through every contingency, but there were always unexpected variables.

As they approached the bedroom window at the rear of the house, Luke strained to listen for any hint of occupation. They'd spotted a faint light in the living room, but that didn't mean jack. Their targets could be anywhere in the house.

Luke stood to the side of the window. He peeked in through a hole in the curtain. An unmade bed sat on one side of the room. Across the room, a dresser vomited clothes from its drawers. Probably Porky's room.

He reached up and popped the screen out of the seal. After setting it on the ground, he slowly pushed back the window. The light scrape of metal on metal set the hair on the back of his neck on end. Other than the occasional chirp of a cricket, the night was silent, as if holding its breath in anticipation of explosive violence.

Boyd laced his fingers together and gave Luke a boost into the room. Luke helped pull Boyd in after him. The door to the bedroom stood open to the hall. They closed the distance and lined up beside it.

Luke pointed to the right. Boyd nodded. Carpet in the empty hallway disguised their steps. As they approached the master bedroom, Luke's heart kicked hard against his ribcage.

"Hey Dad," someone yelled. "Did you hear anything?"

Footsteps sounded from the down the hall. A second pair came from the opposite direction. Trapped between father and son, Luke charged toward the son. He blitzed the chubby bastard, throwing an elbow at his jaw before punching him in the stomach with a sharp jab. Porky gasped and stumbled back against a wall. Luke circled behind and grabbed him by the throat. He put a gun to his head.

"Don't fucking move."

"Who the fuck—"

Bart stepped into the hall. When he pointed his flashlight at Boyd, his jaw dropped.

"Son of a bitch. You're home."

"You're goddammed right. I found my family. They're all dead, and you killed them."

"Let go of my son and get the fuck out of my house."

"You murdered my family!"

"And had a great time doing it." Bart sneered.

Luke yanked on Porky's throat in an attempt to distract his father. He changed the position of the gun, pointing it at Bart instead.

"Up against the wall, hands behind your back," Luke snapped.

"Fuck you!"

Bart turned and dashed back into the bedroom. Boyd raced after him before Luke could tell him to stop. He could be running right into a trap.

Luke smashed the butt of his gun against the side of Porky's head. The hulking giant crumbled to the floor.

After leaping over him, Luke raced toward the bedroom.

A shotgun blast punctured the air. Boyd

screamed. Something thudded against the wall. Luke ran toward the door, hoping he wasn't too late.

A muzzle flash blinded Luke a split second before Bart rushed him. A slug whizzed past his ear. Luke slammed into Bart, dropping his SIG in the process. He grabbed the shotgun and twisted it up toward the ceiling just as another shot blasted free.

As he tried to wrestle it away, Boyd groaned in the corner. Luke couldn't take his eyes off Bart to check on his friend. He pulled as hard as he could, then shoved forward, smacking Bart across the nose. The man howled as blood rushed out of his nose. His grip weakened enough for Luke to tear the gun from his hands.

Behind him, Boyd dragged himself up from the floor via the wall. He staggered toward Luke.

"Hand me the gun."

"I got this," Luke snapped as he pointed the business end at Bart.

He pulled the shotgun and pulled the trigger. It clicked, but nothing happened. He checked the chamber. Empty.

Bart laughed and staggered to his feet. He wiped the back of his hand across his gushing nose. Blood stained his sleeve.

"You know what your wife did when I was

fucking her?" Bart took a shaky step forward. "She cried and begged you to save her."

Out of the corner of his eye, Luke watched Boyd grab the SIG. Everything happened in slow motion. Boyd raised the pistol and advanced with the determination of a militant army. A flash of movement near the door caught Luke's attention. He spun and ran toward Porky's hulking form.

As Porky raised a second shotgun toward Boyd, Luke grabbed the muzzle and shoved it up. The shot reverberated down his arm. He yanked the gun out of Porky's grasp and flipped it around. He pumped it and pulled the trigger, sending a round right through his heart. He dropped.

He spun toward Bart. The muzzle on the pistol in Boyd's hand flashed. As Bart jerked back, blood splattered on the wall behind him. He slammed into the wall and slid to the ground. The sinister glint in his eyes faded until all that remained was a glassy stare.

Boyd put a second bullet between Bart's eyes. The sound of his panting and the reek of cordite filled the room. As the smoke dissipated, Boyd turned to gaze at Luke with a stunned expression.

"He didn't suffer."

"But he's dead. Now he'll never be able to do that to another family."

"I wanted him to suffer the way they did."

"Let's get out of here."

When Boyd didn't move, Luke grabbed his upper arm and pulled him toward the door.

"Wait," Boyd said.

He pulled away from Luke and walked back to where Bart lay against the wall. Boyd spit on his face and kicked his corpse. He kicked the dead man again and again as a primal scream roared from the depths of his soul.

Luke stood back as Boyd dropped to his knees, punching and kicking until he collapsed onto all fours. As he looked up, blood spatter dripped down his face. His inhuman, feral countenance made Luke step back a couple of paces.

"It's done," Boyd said. "Let's go home."

As they headed back to Boyd's house, the adrenaline in Luke's body dissipated, leaving him shaky and exhausted. Without a word, he found a clean spot on the living room floor in Boyd's house, curled into a ball, and fell asleep instantly.

When Luke woke up several hours later, sunlight streamed in through the sliding glass door to warm his face. Every muscle in his body screamed. He groaned and rolled onto his back.

"You up?" Boyd asked as he walked in from the kitchen.

"Yeah."

"I made coffee." Boyd handed a steaming cup to Luke.

The spicy aroma wafted up on trails of steam. The first sip awakened his mind and body. Even though he could have slept for a week straight, the coffee gave him enough energy to face the day.

"I went back to Bart's house at sunrise," Boyd said. "Found some supplies. They've got a six-month stockpile in the kitchen. I can't even imagine how many other families they murdered."

Luke remained silent, unsure of what to say.

"I packed up the beef jerky and I've got some water for you," Boyd said. "I figured you'd want to get on the road soon."

"What are you going to do?"

"Not sure. Clean this place up, I guess. I don't know. I've got nothing left. Nothing more to live for. My family meant everything. Everything."

His shoulders slumped. Although Boyd had gotten revenge, it clearly hadn't been enough. Staying at the house would only increase his pain. But maybe he didn't have to.

Luke tossed an idea around in his head. What if Boyd came with him? They had plenty of food at the cabin and it would be nice to have another person around to defend it. Sleeping quarters would have to be arranged because they didn't have any extra beds, but he'd figure something out. But was it a wise decision?

He'd have another mouth to feed. Even though they had a lot of food stored, adding another person to the mix would cut down on what he could feed his family. They could conceivably head out on supply runs when they needed to, but that would be dangerous. Was it worth the risk?

After taking another sip of coffee, he set up a mental list of pluses and minuses. On the one hand, he'd be in a better position to defend the house. On the other, he'd be bringing a near stranger into the fold. Sure, they'd worked together the last few days to get through the city, but he didn't really know Boyd. The guy could be irritating as hell sometimes. Would he drive him nuts over time?

And what would Liz think? He'd harped on her over and over never to tell anyone about their Bug Out Location, so how could he show up with another person in tow?

He sighed.

"You're thinking so hard there's steam coming out your ears," Boyd said.

"Just trying to puzzle something out."

"What?"

Maybe Boyd wouldn't even want to go with him. Maybe it was a moot point. He'd have to feel him out.

"What are you planning on doing in the long-term?" Luke asked.

Boyd shrugged.

"Do you have any family anywhere else?"

"Colorado."

"It would take months, maybe a year to get to them," Luke said.

"Not something I want to consider."

"What about coming with me?"

"What?"

"Hear me out. I don't have much. It's a small cabin in the woods. We've got a stream running through it, so access to fresh water. I've got some food stored up, but we'd need to look for more, or get a garden set up. Maybe both."

"I can't," Boyd said. "I wouldn't want to impose on your family."

"You wouldn't be. You'd have to do your part, of course."

"I'm not a freeloader."

"I know."

"What would I do all day?" Boyd asked.

"Work on projects that need to get done. Help

keep the cabin secure. We'd have to set up perimeter patrols. Go hunting. Maybe fishing if we can find anything in the lake."

"You've got a lake too?"

"It's not on our property," Luke said. "It's actually a few miles away, but they used to stock it with fish every season. I don't know if there's anything left in there, but it's worth checking it out."

"I'm not afraid of a little work."

"What are you afraid of?"

"You think your wife'll be okay with it? I don't want to walk all the way there and find out she doesn't want me around."

"She'll probably be happy to have another guy around to shout orders at," Luke said with a grin.

"She's a real fishmonger, hmm?"

"Don't let her ever hear you say it. She'd cut off your head. Besides, she wouldn't be the only one with expectations."

"Oh yeah?"

"I'd expect you to work night and day to keep my family in the lifestyle to which they've grown accustomed."

Boyd laughed. "So you're looking for an indentured servant?"

"A butler. A gardener. A security force. Not much."

"Sounds like a dream come true, but I can't. This is my home."

"You already said there's nothing left for you here," Luke said.

"I've still got memories here. Good and bad. I know they're gone, but if I leave this place, I feel like I'd be abandoning my family too."

"You did everything you could for them. What happened wasn't your fault. There's no way you could have known that the whole world would go straight to shit while you were on vacation."

"You keep saying that."

"Because it's the truth."

Boyd clenched his jaw hard enough to make it twitch.

"Think about it," Luke said. "I need a good night's sleep before I go. I'm leaving at sunrise tomorrow. If you want to come with me, be ready to roll at dawn."

22

Liz repositioned Melinda's arms as she dry-fired the rifle. They'd spent the last two hours practicing and she hadn't gotten any better. Her aim sucked. She did have a surprising amount of arm strength though, so at least she wasn't a total disaster.

"Don't shoot," Harvey called from the edge of the forest.

"It's not loaded." Melinda lowered the gun.

"Well there's your first mistake. Ready to head out?"

"Ready." Liz took the gun from her. "I'm going to load it. Remember what I said, don't point it at anyone you don't want dead."

"I don't want to point it at anyone, period."

"You might have to," Liz said. "If you're not ready

for this, you can stay at the cabin. We'll bring the kids back."

"No. I'm coming. I'm ready."

"Okay. Let's go," Harvey said.

They trekked through the forest until they reached the rendezvous position. Burt, Franklin, and their wives were already there. Burt carried a can of gasoline.

"I hate to part with it, but it's the only fuel we could find," Burt said.

"Thank you," Liz said. "I'll find a way to repay you."

"No need. We're all in this together. Some of us might be dragging our feet about it, but eventually everyone will see what I see. If we don't work together, we're totally fucked."

Finally, people were starting to see the truth.

"Let's run through the plan again," Liz said. "Burt lights the fire then circles around to secure the escape route. Melinda and I will go get the kids as soon as the guards leave."

"What if they don't leave?" Franklin asked.

"If they don't leave, I'll shoot them," Liz said.

"In cold blood?"

"They're holding my kids captive. As far as I'm concerned, it's an act of war."

"As long as you can live with your choices..."

Franklin pressed his lips together and gave her a slight nod.

"I have no problem killing to save my kids."

"It's almost time for the shift change," Melinda said. "We need to get into position."

"I'll set the fire in five minutes. Be ready." Burt picked up the gas can and headed through the woods toward the house they'd designated.

"Everyone else, get ready. We don't know where all of the men are or any of their positions," Liz said. "We need to be ready for anything."

The group fanned out. Liz and Melinda walked to the cliff overlooking their target.

"If people start shooting, you have to shoot back," Liz said. "Hesitation could get us killed."

"I know." Her voice trembled. Not good. Maybe she wasn't ready for this, but it was too late now.

The subtle scent of smoke filled the air. In the distance, a dim red glow shined through the trees.

"The guards haven't seen it yet," Melinda whispered.

"Not yet. Give it a minute. Once the firewood catches, it's going to burn fast and hot."

Thirty seconds later, the shrill jangle of a frantically rung bell split the air. People shouted and rushed down the road toward the fire. Flames licked up toward the sky, brightening the tree line.

The guards jumped up from their seated positions and huddled together, as if trying to decide what to do. One man gestured at the door before turning toward the distant fire.

"They're trying to figure out what to do," Liz whispered.

"Leave, dammit."

Two guards jogged down the road toward the fire, leaving one guard standing on the front porch.

"Shit. We still have one."

"Can you take him out from here?" Melinda asked.

"It's too far."

"We need to get rid of him. I'll go down and distract him. I'll tell him Elijah wants him to help put out the fire."

"He'll never fall for that," Liz said.

"If he doesn't, then what?"

"Then you have to shoot him. He's the only thing standing between you and your son. I can't do this for you. You're going to have to do it yourself."

Melinda let out a low groan before shoving her shoulders back. When she turned toward the path to the house, Liz grabbed her shoulder.

"Wait."

"What?" Melinda turned.

"Hesitation will get you killed. If you don't think you can do this..."

"I can do it."

Liz stepped back as Melinda headed toward the house. When she stepped out of the forest, the guard turned toward her. His hand rested on the pistol at his waist. She started gesturing wildly and pointed toward the fire. The guard cocked his head to one side. They appeared to argue for several seconds before he finally took off toward the fire.

Elated, Liz ran down the hill. She met Melinda at the back window.

"This kids aren't near this window, right?" Liz asked as she hoisted the rifle overhead.

"No. They're in the kitchen."

"Get back."

Melinda jumped back as Liz used the butt of the gun to smash the window. After knocking all of the glass out of the way, she reached up and pulled herself inside. Sierra, Kyle, and Adam whipped their heads around to stare at her with wide eyes.

"Mom!" Sierra jerked against the chair. "Where are the guards?"

"We took care of them. Don't move while I cut you free." Liz pulled a knife out of her pocket and flipped the blade out. She sawed at the ropes around Sierra's ankles first.

"I knew you'd come," Adam said.

"I'd never leave you." Melinda dropped to the floor to cut the rope off of his ankles.

After quickly slicing through all of the ropes, Kyle flung himself into Liz's arms.

"I thought they were going to kill us," he said.

"We're not safe yet. We need to get out of here." Liz ran toward the front door and checked the peephole. No one was outside. "When I say go, run into the forest and wait for us. We have other people out there, so don't scream if you see them. We need to be as quiet as possible. Go!"

Sierra, Kyle, and Adam raced toward the forest. Liz motioned for Melinda to go next.

As Liz ran toward the forest, the first shots rang out. They were coming from somewhere down the road. She grabbed the rifle and returned fire. Additional cover fire burst from the forest, giving her the break she needed to get inside the tree line.

"This way," Harvey yelled at the kids.

Everyone ran deeper into the forest toward the route they'd pre-planned. As they raced through an open meadow, bullets sliced through the air.

"Take cover. Get back into the trees," Liz yelled.

She scrambled behind a huge oak and jammed the butt of the rifle against her shoulder. She opened up, cutting down two men before stopping to reload.

Franklin stood three feet away behind another tree. He shot two more men before being hit in the shoulder. He dropped his gun and fell back against the tree.

"Run! I'll cover you." Liz leaned out enough to get a clear shot and fired. She narrowly missed one man who turned and ran back into the forest.

"Move out."

Liz backed away from the tree. When she turned to run, she found herself ten steps away from the preacher. He pointed a revolver at her chest and smiled.

"Drop the gun."

She tossed it at his feet.

"I should have shot you the first time I met you." He cocked the hammer. "I suspected you'd started the fire so I sent a group into the forest. You're not as smart as you think you are."

"Fuck you."

"That filthy mouth." Elijah shook his head. "You know what your problem is?"

"No. Tell me." Liz wanted to keep him talking, anything to buy time.

"You don't know your place. You should have submitted to a husband. A woman like you, alone, gets all kinds of ideas. Dangerous ideas."

A man shoved Franklin to the ground beside her.

He groaned and doubled over. Blood soaked the sleeve on one shoulder.

"Where are the brats?" Elijah snapped.

"They got away."

Relief rushed through her so fast she felt light-headed. She might end up dead, but at least Harvey and the others could keep her kids safe until Luke came home.

She closed her eyes and sent up a silent prayer. She didn't know how she was going to get out of this alive, but as long as she could take a breath, she'd keep fighting.

In all of the chaos, Sierra lost the others. She stopped and hid behind a tree. An unintelligible conversation drifted from somewhere in the woods. She strained to make out the voices. When she recognized Elijah and her mom's voices, she crept closer. She didn't have a weapon, but she'd have to figure something out.

As she slid around a tree, she spotted Melinda hiding behind an oak across from her. Sierra frowned at the way Melinda held her rifle. It was all wrong and she wouldn't have a shot in hell at hitting a target.

Sierra waved her arms and tried to get her attention. If she could get the gun from Melinda, she'd be able to take the preacher out. Being held in the house for almost twenty-four hours had stoked her rage to a new level. Her trigger finger itched to put a bullet in the preacher's head.

When Melinda finally spotted her, Sierra gestured toward the rifle. Melinda took a step out from behind a tree. A bullet whizzed past her. She jumped back.

"Throw it to me," Sierra yelled. No point in trying to hide their location since they were already under fire.

Melinda tossed the gun, but it landed three feet short.

"Fuck."

Sierra waited until the shooter finished a magazine before scrambling out from hiding. She grabbed the rifle and dove behind the tree, narrowly escaping the first shots out of the shooter's fresh magazine.

"Asshole!"

She inched around the edge of the tree and took a quick look. The shooter stood with his back to the growing firelight, giving her a perfect target. She aimed for center mass and shot. He jerked back and fell to the ground. She ran forward, kicked his rifle to the side and put another shot through his head.

A bullet smashed into a tree to her right. She dashed forward and hid behind another tree. Her breath came in short gasps as she scanned the forest. A branch snapped ten yards to her right. She inched toward the left, carefully picking her way past small branches.

When she missed and stepped on a twig, the resulting crack gave away her location. The shooter annihilated the tree with bullets. Pieces of bark burst out to form projectiles. Several chunks landed in her hair.

"Come out, you little bitch, or I'll kill your mother," the preacher said.

Sierra risked a glance around the tree. The preacher held a gun to her mom's head.

"Don't listen to him," her mom said. "He'll kill us both. Run!"

The preacher slammed the butt of the gun into her mom's head. Her mom crumpled to the ground. As he pulled the hammer on the gun back, Sierra took aim and fired.

The bullet tore through the preacher's shoulder. He stumbled back a few steps before firing off a wild shot.

Sierra shot him again, and again, making him dance like a spastic marionette until the mag ran out. When he fell to the ground, she screamed and ran forward. She yanked the revolver out of his hand and pointed it at his face.

"I hope you enjoy hell."

She pulled the trigger, putting a bullet directly between his eyes. Light flickered in his eyes before fading. The crazed expression on his face relaxed into a blank expression as death claimed him.

Sierra shoved the gun in her pocket and ran toward her mom.

"Mom?"

Liz groaned and tried to sit up.

"Don't move."

"There are more," Liz mumbled.

"How many? Where?"

"Don't know."

"We got them." Harvey ran up to them. "We killed them all."

"Everyone from the church?" Sierra asked.

"No. Just the ones shooting at us. Everyone else fled. Some are still trying to put out the fire." Harvey walked over to Elijah and checked for a pulse. "He'd dead."

"I killed him," she whispered. "He hit my mom with the gun."

"You did the right thing. We need to get her back to the cabin. She probably has a concussion."

Franklin and several others from their group jogged up. As Harvey and Franklin moved to pick up her semiconscious mom, Sierra dropped to her knees.

An overwhelming weight pressed her into the ground. She'd just killed a man. The absolute horror of watching the light in his eyes fade replayed over and over until she couldn't see anything else.

"I think she's going into shock," someone said.

Bile rushed up from her belly. She lunged forward, vomiting nothing but water. She dry-heaved until someone started rubbing her back. She turned her glassy gaze on Adam, who scooped her into his arms.

"I've got you," he murmured. "I'm taking you home."

Sierra went limp as darkness pressed in from every side, eventually rendering her unconscious.

23

Luke rolled up the sleeping bag Boyd had lent him for the night and set it on the coffee table in the living room. Even though the sun peeked over the eastern horizon, the air remained chilly and still. This morning was much colder than the previous day. Cold enough to make him wish he'd stolen a jacket from one of the clothing stores they'd passed several days earlier.

He hadn't spoken to Boyd since their conversation about leaving. He'd been too exhausted to get up for anything beyond a trip to the bathroom. Even now, after almost twelve hours of uninterrupted sleep, he could have crawled back in for another twenty-four.

As he walked into the kitchen, Boyd strolled in

from the hall. He carried a pack on his back and had a jacket in his hand. He'd changed into fresh clothes and had somehow managed to wash up a bit. He'd also shaved. At least he'd look somewhat presentable if he decided to come to the cabin. Although he had his pack on, it didn't mean anything without confirmation.

"I figure we could make a thermos of coffee before we head out," Boyd said.

"You're coming?"

"If the offer still stands."

Luke held out his hand. Boyd grabbed it with a firm grip and shook it.

"Well, now that we've got that all worked out," Boyd said. "We need to decide who gets to be the pack mule."

"I only plan on carrying what I can hold in my pack."

"Well now, that might be a problem."

"Why?"

"Because I loaded up a couple of wheelbarrows full of food, courtesy of those assholes across the street. At first I wasn't going to touch their shit, but then I decided since it wasn't theirs to begin with, I might as well make use of it."

"We're about twenty miles from my house. I can't imagine pushing a wheelbarrow that far. It'll double the amount of time it's going to take to get there."

"But it will stretch out the food supply by another couple of months," Boyd said. "I think losing a day in transit is worth it."

Luke sighed. He had a point. But they'd already taken the extra day to rest. Now that he was back on his feet, he was ready to do the whole twenty miles today, if possible. He wouldn't be able to making the entire journey in one day while pushing a wheelbarrow around.

"Let's just try it," Boyd said. "Worst case scenario, we ditch the supplies somewhere and go back for them."

"All right."

After a breakfast of hot coffee and chili, courtesy of a camping stove, Luke slipped his pack on.

"Did you ever find your gun over at the other house?" Luke asked.

"No. Never did find where they put it. But I did find the ammo. It's in one of the wheelbarrows. It's mostly 9mm, but I found a box of shotgun shells too. There's about eighty rounds of 9mm and twenty-five slugs."

"I need to reload."

"Be my guest. We don't have anything else to put the 9mm in. Those bastards. I loved my Taurus 85."

"Small gun."

"It'd still put a hole right through you. And I could hide it pretty much anywhere."

"I don't want to know all the places you used to hide it," Luke said with a smirk.

"Smart ass."

"Okay, let's try the wheelbarrows. If they get to be too much of a pain in the ass though, we have to ditch them."

"Works for me. Everything in them would be a good bonus, but if you're already stocked up…"

"Food for at least a year. Maybe eight months with you there."

"Six if you're lucky."

"Don't make me rethink this."

"I wouldn't dream of it."

As they headed out the front door, Boyd turned to lock it. He hesitated with the key in his hand.

"Guess I don't need to lock it anymore."

"Not really."

"We lived here twenty years. Raised the kids here. Thought we'd grow old together and die in this little house. I guess I got the dying part right and the timeline wrong."

Luke shook his head slightly.

"Maybe I'll be back one day," Boyd said as he slid the key into the lock and turned it.

The trip through the neighborhood proved to be uneventful. Luke hated to think about how many other families lay massacred in their homes. Two weeks ago he never would have dreamed of walking down the middle of a four-lane road. There wasn't a single car in sight. No people either.

At one point they had to push the wheelbarrows up an off-ramp on the 91 Freeway. As they headed toward the 241 Toll Road, Luke shivered.

"Does it feel like it's getting colder to you?" he asked.

"It never warmed up. The sky looks funny too. Gray, but there aren't any clouds."

"Yeah, it's weird."

"Do you think there's a fire someplace?"

"I haven't smelled any smoke."

"Me neither," Boyd said. "Maybe up in LA though. After they nuked Hiroshima, the whole city burned down."

"I hope that didn't happen in LA. I've got a HAM radio at the cabin."

"Maybe we'll be able to get some news."

"Maybe."

After pushing the wheelbarrows all day, Luke's arms were ready to fall off. The sun rested low on the horizon as they reached a fork in the Toll Road. One section continued, while the other became an off-ramp to Santiago Canyon Road. As Luke heaved the load up the steep off-ramp, his calf muscles screamed. Boyd huffed behind him until they reached the top of the grade.

"Are we there yet?" Boyd joked.

"You sound like one of my kids."

"Mine used to say it all the time." A far-off expression crossed his face.

Luke set the wheelbarrow down and pulled a bottle of water out of his pack. He took a long swig before setting it back on the pile. As he reached for a Snickers bar, Boyd turned his back. His chin sagged toward his chest for a moment before he heaved his head to each side to crack his neck. When he turned around, his red-rimmed eyes reflected the sunset.

"It's all I think about," he said.

"I know."

"No. You don't. You still have your family," he said softly, without bitterness.

"I hope so. I'd give anything to be able to call them."

"About how far do we have to go?"

"Maybe another eight to ten miles."

"We still have another hour of light or so. I found a couple of headlamps at the house. They're in my wheelbarrow when we need them. I figure we'll keep on through the night."

"Aren't you exhausted?" Luke asked.

"Yeah, but if I was this close to my family, a pack of wild hyenas couldn't keep me away."

"Let's do it then."

After finishing off the bottle of water, Luke tossed it back onto the pile. About two miles up the road, Luke pointed to a lake.

"That's the one I was talking about. The water's really low from the drought and they stopped stocking it with fish, but there might still be some."

"We can check it out after we get settled. That's an easy day trip, even on foot."

As darkness stretched across the rolling hills, Boyd pulled the headlamps out. He handed one to Luke.

"If anyone's out here, they'll be able to see us from a mile away."

"It's kind of weird we haven't run into anyone considering how many people live around this area."

"I wonder why."

"Maybe because of that?"

Luke squinted against the night. Up ahead, four men carrying rifles stood across the road. Great. Just what he needed. It was too late to dash into the trees. They'd already been seen for sure. Since they hadn't started shooting already, maybe they weren't standing around waiting to kill people. Or maybe they were. Either way, he was about to find out.

LIZ GINGERLY TOUCHED the knot on her forehead. She sat at the kitchen table in her cabin. Adam sat across from her while Melinda poured three steaming cups of tea. She carried the mugs to the table and passed them out. Liz took a shaky sip before setting the cup down. She glanced at the ceiling. Kyle lay sleeping in the loft. Sierra had locked herself in the bedroom and was refusing to come out.

"Are they sure everyone's dead?" Liz asked.

"Harvey and the others went back. They rounded up everyone left at the church and demanded to know who else was involved in the kidnapping. No one knew anything," Melinda said.

"And they believed them?"

"Yes. The people were unbelievably clueless. I never understood how no one could see him for what he really was." Melinda shook her head.

"No one knew the preacher was kidnapping and murdering people?"

"No. And if they suspected, they probably ignored their suspicions. People want to believe the best about the powerful people around them. The alternative is too horrifying to imagine. If I'd told people my suspicions about Elijah, no one would have believed me. Before the bombs, it happened all the time. All kinds of atrocities happened, but a single voice doesn't stand a chance against powerful people."

Liz nodded slightly. She stopped as a band of pain tightened around her forehead.

"You need to rest," Melinda said.

"We don't have much room, but please stay here tonight. We'll figure out something more permanent tomorrow."

"Permanent?" Adam raised his head.

"I know you don't really have a place to go, so unless you're planning on rebuilding the church group..."

"I don't ever want to go back there," Adam said.

"You don't have to," Melinda said. "I appreciate your offer, but I don't know if we're ready to join another group yet."

"Consider it," Liz said. "In the meantime, you're welcome to stay with us as long as you want."

They sipped tea in silence for several minutes.

"I should check on Sierra," Liz said.

"Leave her be for now," Melinda said. "She's in shock. She killed a man. She watched him die. You don't get over something like that after a couple of hours."

"How are you holding up?" Liz asked.

"I did what I had to do to save my son." Melinda dropped her gaze to the mug and studied its contents as if she were trying to divine the future. "I never thought I'd take a life."

"Mom," Adam grabbed his mom's hand and squeezed. "You could have run away, but you didn't. You stayed and you fought for me."

"I love you more than anything in the world," Melinda choked.

"I love you too, Mom."

Liz looked at the front door and sighed. No one would be the same after tonight. Would Luke even recognize them when he made it home?

Her heart clenched as Melinda and Adam leaned against each other. Family meant everything, but right now Liz's wasn't complete. Not until Luke came home.

"I'm going to check on Sierra."

She pushed back from the table and walked to the bedroom door. She knocked softly.

"Go away," Sierra called from inside.

"Unlock the door."

"It is unlocked."

Liz twisted the doorknob and slipped inside. She sat on the edge of the bed and reached for Sierra's hand. She rolled away.

"I know tonight was a nightmare," Liz said. "But you did everything right. We're alive."

"None of this would have happened if I'd listened

to you in the first place. You warned me not to talk to other people, but I did it anyway."

"You made a mistake."

"And now people are dead. Everyone died today because of me."

"No one from our group died. Franklin's going to be all right. He was hit in the shoulder, but they patched him up. He'll be fine in a few weeks," Liz said.

"You should have seen the look in his eyes when he died. It was like staring into hell."

"I'm sorry you had to do that, but you were the only one who could save me. You had to do it."

"I don't want to talk about it," Sierra said.

"Okay." Liz didn't want to push her too hard. It would take time to process everything, and eventually Sierra would realize she had no choice but to pull the trigger.

She tucked Sierra in, then closed the door. Melinda and Adam had moved into the living room. Melinda lay on one of the couches, while Adam sat on the other.

"Try to get some sleep," Liz said.

"What about you?" Adam asked.

"I can't sleep. Harvey checked and doesn't think I have a concussion, but I should stay up just in case."

"I'll stay up with you."

"No. Rest. I'll be fine."

As Liz padded toward the kitchen, a perimeter bell rang. She froze. Adam jumped up and quickly crossed the room to peek out the curtains.

"I don't see anyone."

"Wait here." Liz grabbed a shotgun and stalked toward the door. "Don't come out until I give the all-clear."

Liz shivered as she reached for the doorknob. She'd thought all the men were dead, but maybe she'd been wrong.

24

Luke set the wheelbarrow down twenty feet in front of the men on the road. He needed his hands free in case he needed to draw on them. He didn't want to reveal that they had a gun unless necessary. The shotgun lay hidden underneath a blanket in Boyd's wheelbarrow. He'd had the foresight to load it before heading out that morning.

"Hello," Luke called as he approached the men.

The man standing on the far left side stepped forward. He wore jeans, a pair of well-worn tennis shoes, and a backward baseball hat. Mid-thirties, relatively fit, but Luke could probably take him in a fistfight. A gunfight? Maybe. Depended on who was fastest to the trigger.

"What's your business here?"

"Just heading home," Luke said.

"Where's that?"

"Up in the canyon."

"Which one?"

"White Oak," he lied. Until he could figure out their intent, he wasn't about to give them a damn bit of information.

"You got a cabin up there?"

"Yep. How about you guys, you up in one of the canyons too?"

"We're at the church."

"Up Modjeska Canyon?"

"Yeah."

"I've been there a few times." Long enough to realize the congregation wasn't a good fit for him. Too literal for his taste.

"What's in the wheelbarrows?"

"Some supplies for the house."

"You're gonna have to pay a toll."

"A toll? I have every right to be on this road, same as you. Why would I have to pay a toll?" Luke demanded.

"Consider it a tax for keeping people who don't belong up here out. I'm also gonna need to see some ID."

"I lost it." Somewhere on the Pacific Crest Trail the damn thing had fallen out of his pocket. Probably a blessing in disguise since they wouldn't be able to get his address.

"We can't let you past unless you got a license with your address on it."

"This is bullshit."

One of the other men trained his rifle on Luke.

"Watch your mouth, buddy." He sounded like he'd been chewing on glass all day.

"Look, I'm just trying to get home to my family."

"Make him pay the toll," Glass-Chewer said.

The man who seemed to be in charge spit on the side of the road.

"Here's what we'll do. You give us one of those wheelbarrows, and we'll let you keep the other one."

Luke clenched his hands into fists. If these assholes thought they were going to take his stuff, they had another thing coming. If only he could figure out how to turn the tables on the situation. They were outnumbered. He glanced at Boyd who shrugged.

As much as Luke wanted to retain everything they'd been pushing around all day, there was no way they'd get past these guys. If they tried to backtrack, these guys would gun them down and take everything. They may have been from the church, but that didn't mean they were men of the cloth. Far from it. He'd bet his left nut they'd broken at least five out of the Ten Commandments in the last week. They had that look.

"Okay," Luke said with an exaggerated sigh. "I just want to get home, so take my friend's wheelbarrow."

"We'd rather have yours," the leader said.

"You could at least let me choose."

"The choice has been made. Rusty, go get it." He turned back to Luke. "Now you boys have a nice rest of your day."

"Asshole," Boyd whispered under his breath.

"What'd you say?"

"Nothing."

"I thought so."

"Let's go," Luke said.

A mile up the road, Boyd turned to him.

"What the hell did you do that for?"

"They were going to take the stuff either way. I figured we might have a chance to salvage one if we gave them the other one."

"You're lucky they didn't take the one with the shotgun."

"Not lucky, smart. I knew they'd pick whichever one I tried to keep, so I made it seem like I wanted mine so we could keep yours. Either way, we still have more than what we came with."

"I don't like it," Boyd said.

"Neither do I, but there's no way in hell I'm getting myself shot this close to home. They said they're with the church. Trust me when I say we're getting every bit of what they took back, and then some. Those sons of bitches don't know what they started."

"Damn straight."

"The turnoff is coming up. We've only got one wheelbarrow left. I'm thinking we should stash it somewhere in case we run into another group. They might have circles of protection around their territory. See those oaks over there? We could stash the wheelbarrow and come back for the supplies tomorrow."

"Okay."

Boyd rolled the wheelbarrow down the embankment and across an open space. When he reached a grove of oak trees, Luke pointed.

"Over there, behind those bushes."

"Can you see the road from here?"

"No. But… I think they may have been following us."

"What?" Boyd craned his neck. "It's getting too dark to see anything."

"Hopefully they didn't watch us go down here."

"I think we should find another spot, just in case."

"Let me check. I've still got my monocular," Luke said.

"I'm surprised they didn't go for our packs."

"They probably thought the wheelbarrows had better stuff."

"They could have shot us and taken anything. Why didn't they?"

"Maybe they want to follow us back to the house and take everything." Luke lifted the monocular to one eye. Night switched to day. Trees and large boulders stood out like light gray sentinels against the darker sky. With a two-hundred-yard view in every direction, it didn't take long to locate their tail. One guy was up on the road looking back and forth.

"He's up there," Luke whispered.

"Let me see."

Luke handed him the monocular.

"We're pinned down."

"No. He doesn't have any night vision gear on. If we wait until full dark, we won't be able to see our hands in front of our faces out here."

"Okay."

Impatience tightened Luke's spine. He was less than an hour away from the cabin. He could hardly wait to see Liz. The moment he had her in his arms, he'd kiss her until she melted. And the kids? God, he'd swing them around like they were still two years old. They were the light of his life. If anything had happened to them while he was gone, he'd never forgive himself. He could understand why Boyd still held onto his guilt. Rationally, he knew if anything happened, he wouldn't be to blame. But emotionally, it would destroy him.

After an hour of waiting around, he tapped Boyd on the shoulder.

"Looks like that guy headed back to the group. It's clear for now," Luke said.

"Keep your eyes peeled."

"I'm scanning."

"Lead the way."

Luke climbed back onto the road. He checked both directions to make sure their tail was gone. After crossing the road, they headed up the canyon road. Each step added to his excitement. And by the time he reached the turnoff to the cabin, he couldn't hold back. He jogged up to the gate across the road.

As he tried to walk around it, his foot caught on a tripwire. Bells jangled as he stumbled forward. He put out a hand to catch himself and landed on a sharp spike.

"Fuck!"

"What happened?" Boyd asked.

"Traps. Watch out."

"Traps?"

"Don't you fucking move!" a woman growled.

The click-clack of a shotgun being racked strangled his breath.

"Luke?" Liz dropped the shotgun and flung herself into his arms. "Oh my God. Oh my God."

He clung to her, smothering her with a kiss borne of two weeks of pure desperation. The struggle, the pain, the suffering, and the miles and miles of fear had been worth it. She melted into the kiss, returning his passion with her own, untethered need, as if to reaffirm his presence.

As he pulled her close, the intoxicating scent of pine and hope mingled to awaken his soul. Now that they were together, anything was possible. They'd survive the apocalypse. No, more than survive—they'd thrive. They had everything they needed to stay alive for a year. Even with Boyd in tow, they'd have enough to make it.

When Boyd cleared his throat, Liz stiffened in Luke's arms.

"Who's there?"

"His name's Boyd. I met him on the road. We traveled together through most of the Inland Empire."

"Nice to meet you," Boyd said.

"I thought we agreed not to bring anyone here,"

she whispered, as if Boyd weren't standing two feet away.

"He lost his entire family. He's a good man and I thought maybe we could use the extra help around the cabin. We've got plenty of food."

"No, we don't."

"What do you mean, what happened?"

"A lot… I don't even know where to begin," she said.

"We'll figure it out. Once we get settled and I've had time to let this leg heal—"

"What happened to your leg? Dammit, it's too dark to see anything right now. Let's go inside."

"Okay."

When Boyd didn't move to follow them, Luke turned back. "You coming?"

"Ah, I don't want to go where I'm not welcome," Boyd said. "I could turn around and go home."

"Not happening," Luke said. "You're staying with us. Come on."

"Your wife doesn't want me here," Boyd said.

"She doesn't know you. I don't blame her. I'd be wary of a stranger too."

"Okay," Boyd said. "But if she really doesn't want me to stay, I'll leave. You just say the word and I'm gone."

"I won't ask you to leave." When Boyd didn't respond, Luke nodded. "Okay, it's settled."

Liz stood on the porch.

"I don't know where we're going to fit everyone," she said. "We have other guests."

"Who?" Luke asked.

"I'll explain everything."

Liz knocked on the door three times. After a brief scraping sound, the door swung open.

"Adam, I'd like you to meet Luke, my husband."

"It's nice to meet you sir." He offered his hand.

As Luke shook it, Melinda sat up on one of the couches. She stood and joined them.

"This is Adam's mom, Melinda. They helped us when—"

Kyle appeared at the top of the stairs.

"Dad?" He rubbed his eyes. "Dad!"

Kyle launched himself at Luke, nearly knocking him over in the process. After steadying himself, Luke grabbed his son and held him so tight that Kyle squealed in protest.

"Ouch," Kyle gasped.

"Shit. Sorry. I'm just so glad to see you. Are you okay?"

"I'm fine, but the preacher took Sierra. He—"

"Who? What do you mean he took her?"

"It's a long story."

"What preacher? Where is she?"

"She's in the bedroom." When he took a step toward it, Liz grabbed his hand. "Wait. We have a lot to talk about before you go in there."

Liz closed the front door and slid a two by four into place. A single candle illuminated the space. A stockpile of weapons sat in one corner of the room. Embers from a dying fire popped in the fireplace.

"Is Sierra okay?" he asked

"She's sleeping. I'll make tea."

"I want to see her."

"She's not...she's not ready to see anyone. And she needs to rest. Come sit down."

Luke glanced at the closed bedroom door before heading toward the kitchen table. As much as he wanted to see her, he could wait a few hours. He trusted Liz. If she said he should wait, he would, even though it tore at his heart.

"Melinda and Adam, if you want to go back to sleep, go ahead." Liz set a kettle on the stove. "I'll fill them in."

"Boyd?" Luke slid into a seat at the kitchen table and indicated Boyd should do the same. He took the seat across from Luke.

"I've got tea and hot chocolate," Liz said.

"Hot chocolate?" Boyd's eyes lit up.

"I'll have some too," Luke said.

After Liz set the steaming mugs in front of them, Luke took a sip. He sat back in his chair.

"What happened while I was gone?" he asked.

"A lot. I don't even know where to start."

"Tell me everything."

As Liz launched into an animated retelling of the last two weeks, a dark cloud of anger took residence in his body. This preacher guy had attacked his family. He'd taken his daughter and subjected her to God knew what. He'd pay. Luke would make him pay. No one fucked with his family.

"Did you hear what I said? Sierra killed him."

"What?" Luke looked up as thoughts of vengeance evaporated.

"When we were fleeing, the preacher captured me. He was going to kill me, but Sierra shot him. She watched him die."

"Jesus." Luke reached for his wife's hand. He held it and never wanted to let go. "What about the other men?"

"Dead. We killed all of them."

"I have to see my daughter." He couldn't wait. He couldn't imagine the emotional turmoil she must be going through.

Liz's lips formed a thin line, but she nodded.

Luke walked to the bedroom door. As he cracked it open, Sierra rolled over on the bed.

"Sierra," he whispered. "It's Dad. Can I come in?"

"Dad?" She jumped up and ran into his arms. "Thank God you're here."

"I'm home, honey. I'm sorry I wasn't here to protect you."

She burst into tears, clinging to him the way she'd done on her first day of kindergarten. At nineteen years old, she still needed her daddy.

"I did terrible things," she whispered.

"Whatever you did, you did it to survive. That's all that matters."

"Mom hates me."

"She loves you."

"I put us all in danger. I should have known better."

"It's all in the past. We're together now. We're stronger than anything anyone wants to throw our way."

"I killed him." She sobbed. "I had to."

"I know. Mom told me everything. You did the right thing. I'm proud of you."

She continued to cry as she perched on the edge of the bed. He sighed and ran a hand through his hair. Based on experience, he knew there wasn't anything you could do to console someone after their first kill. Justified or not, she'd be traumatized for a long time.

"Where's the compound?" he asked.

"Across the river, over the next ridge. Why?"

"I want to see it."

"No!" Her eyes went wide. "You can't go over there. It's not safe."

"But the preacher's dead. Your mom said everyone who was involved with him is dead."

"They think they got everyone, but how do they know for sure? How do they know more of them aren't hiding out, waiting to strike?" Her wild, unfocused gaze bounced around the room.

"I trust your mom. If she says they're all dead, then they're all dead. I just want to take a look."

"No, Daddy. You can't go." She grabbed his arm.

After gently wrestling it away, he headed back toward the door.

"Get some sleep. We'll talk again in the morning."

He walked into the kitchen.

"I want to see it."

"I can take you there at sunrise. I'm too tired to make the trip now."

"Are you sure they're all dead?" Luke asked.

"Harvey and Franklin seemed to think so."

"The neighbors were there too?"

"We started a community," Liz said. "I'll take you to meet everyone later today."

"They might not all be dead," Boyd said. "We ran

into a group of guys up the road. They claimed they were from a church."

"It's the only one around," Liz said. "They sent groups out in every direction either to guard the road or find more supplies. The men you ran into were probably from the church. I didn't think about the groups that were away from the church when everything went down."

"They stole half our stuff," Boyd said. "If they're back at the church, we'll take care of them before they become a problem."

"You're lucky they didn't kill you," Liz said.

"Boyd, if you're up for it, do you want to come with me?" Luke asked.

"Let me finish my hot chocolate and I'll be ready for anything."

"I don't want you to go," Liz said. "If those other men returned to the church, it's not safe. I just got you back. I don't want to lose you."

"We'll be careful," Luke said. "We'll just take a look. We won't engage anyone."

"I promise I'll bring him back in one piece," Boyd said.

Liz sighed. "Okay, but be careful. Take guns with you."

After grabbing a couple of rifles and extra magazines, Luke and Boyd headed toward the door. He stayed alert as they moved through the forest. The occasional scamper of a squirrel and the hoot of a lone owl were the only sounds in the night. He followed Liz's directions until he reached an overlook.

Luke's jaw twitched as he stood at the edge of the forest. Although most of the preacher's compound lay in smoldering shambles, several men sifted through the rubble. They placed useable items several feet from the fire. They weren't leaving, and as long as they stayed in the canyon, his family would never be safe. Tomorrow, he'd formulate a plan for dealing with them, but for now, he turned around, and headed home.

Three days later, Luke found his daughter's dead body partially buried beneath a shroud of snow.

NEWSLETTER

Don't miss the next book in the American Fallout series: *Edge of Fear*. Want to know when it's coming out? What to find out if Luke ever makes it home or if Liz is able to defend the cabin?

My newsletter subscribers will be the first to find out about the new release. Sometimes I'll send out cover reveals and sneak peaks of chapters from the next book.

Sign up at www.alexgunwick.com

Please consider leaving a review. Authors rely on honest reviews to help spread the word. Readers like you are what makes it possible for me to continue writing edge of your seat suspense books. You don't have to write a huge paragraph, a few words is plenty. I'd really appreciate it.

I never give away email addresses. I personally hate spam so I would never sell your email.

ABOUT THE AUTHOR

Alex Gunwick started researching post-apocalyptic scenarios for book ideas. When she realized how unprepared she and her husband were for a disaster, she launched into prepping. Now she's armed and sitting on enough beans to rocket her to the moon and back. She's already mastered her Mossberg 500 and can't wait to put her HK P2000 through its paces at the range.

Her fantasy of moving to Montana to live in a cabin in the woods has become an obsession. Her husband's totally on board and can't wait to wrangle grizzly bears with his bare hands. We'll see how that works out. ;)

To find out more about her including what she's shooting these days, visit her online at:

www.AlexGunwick.com
AlexGunwick@gmail.com
Facebook.com/AlexGunwick

Made in the USA
Las Vegas, NV
07 February 2025